THE HILLS OF HOPE

Also by Colleen L. Reece
in Large Print:

Alpine Meadows Nurse
Come Home, Nurse Jenny
Everlasting Melody
The Heritage of Nurse O'Hara
In Search of Twilight
Mysterious Monday
Nurse Julie's Sacrifice
Yellowstone Park Nurse

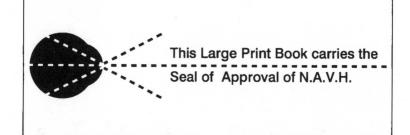

This Large Print Book carries the
Seal of Approval of N.A.V.H.

THE HILLS OF HOPE

COLLEEN L. REECE

Thorndike Press • Thorndike, Maine

Published in 2001 by arrangement with Colleen L. Reece

Thorndike Press Large Print Christian Fiction Series.

The tree indicium is a trademark of Thorndike Press.

The text of this Large Print edition is unabridged.
Other aspects of the book may vary from the original edition.

Set in 16 pt. Plantin by Elena Picard.

Printed in the United States on permanent paper.

Library of Congress Cataloging-in-Publication Data

Reece, Colleen L.
    The hills of hope / by Colleen L. Reece.
      p. cm.
    ISBN 0-7862-3071-1 (lg. print : hc : alk. paper)
    1. World War, 1914–1918 — France — Fiction.
2. Americans — France — Fiction. 3. Washington (State)
— Fiction. 4. Stepfamilies — Fiction. 5. Large type books.
I. Title.
PS3568.E3646 H5 2001
  813′.54—dc21   00-048906

To Mom, the best World War I
research person, manuscript proofer,
and editor an author could find.

1

A low rumble. A faint screech. The whine of wheels on steel rails shining blood red in the early morning sunrise. A long, mournful whistle preceded a belching monster that left a trail of black smoke in its wake and a cloud of black fear over the crowd at the little Dale station. White-faced mothers clung to stripling sons, some barely past boyhood. Sisters and sweethearts silently prayed, their hearts too filled to speak. Farmers turned soldiers who had never been farther from the little Washington village than Seattle or Tacoma grimly waited to board the train that would carry them to Camp Lewis. But their final destination was Europe, a maze of borders, rivers, and dots in their geography books, now the site of a political imbroglio better known as World War I.

Not all the men who waited to serve their country were young. Veterans of the Spanish-American War who had cheered Teddy Roosevelt and his Rough Riders in the

Battle of San Juan Hill would do no less than defend their country against its new enemy. The former battle cry, "Remember the *Maine*," had changed to "Remember the *Lusitania*."

The holiday spirit that had seen other boys and men off to make short work of the Huns had no place in mid-August, 1917. Dale had already turned out en masse for three funerals. The little church had overflowed with tears and anger at Kaiser Wilhelm II, emperor of Germany and warmonger. Even the splendid patriotism and determination of America's finest could not easily end the battle.

A little to one side of the grouped families, nineteen-year-old Hope Farrell raised pleading, amber eyes to her tall companion. One gloved hand rested on his arm. "Do you have to go?"

Timothy Wainwright's intense dark eyes, the same shade as his curly hair, never wavered. "You know I do."

"Even though Father threatens to disown you if you go?"

"Even then." The curl of his fine lips softened and he pressed his arm and her hand closer to his side. "You know I've only waited until I turned twenty-one in the hope he'd ..." His mouth twisted again. "Not that it made any difference. Not that anything I've ever done met with his approval."

Hope stood silent, unable to offer a protest against his bitterness yet longing to erase the lines no man so young should have etched in his face. "Perhaps when he sees how brave you are. . . ." Her voice died. It would take a miracle for Justin Farrell to admit anything good about the stepson he had acquired years before from a second marriage.

"If it hadn't been for Luther maybe things would have been different," she suggested and felt his muscles ripple under her hand.

"Luther!" Timothy spat the hated name between clenched lips. Sparks went off in the dark eyes and he gave a look that made Hope shiver in spite of the warm morning.

"Timothy, *please*. Don't go into battle with this terrible hatred." Her fingers tightened on his arm. "I'll be praying for you the whole time you're gone but how can I expect God to take care of you when you won't acknowledge Him in your life? If you'd just let Jesus into your heart and life you could go overseas with peace that is beyond human understanding!"

Her stepbrother shrugged. "I can't see that God has ever done anything for me."

Cut to her soul by his indifference, Hope

9

cried out in a low voice, "Don't say that! God loves you. If you had been the only person who ever lived, God would still have sent Jesus so you could know Him and have everlasting life." A warning whistle blasted in the fresh morning air. "There's still time, Timothy. It only takes a minute to get right before God and claim His promises. Otherwise there's no hope. *Don't go without it.*"

Timothy bit his lip and averted his gaze. He threw back his head and looked at the still-white mountain peaks beyond them. "I have hope. While I'm gone I'll think of those mountains, how they've stood there for years." He took a deep breath. "They're my hills — and yours. The hills of Hope."

She nodded so vigorously a soft blond lock escaped from her hat and bounced against her cheek. Remembering the hikes and picnics they'd shared did little to allay her frantic thoughts. "Hills and memories aren't enough. You need Jesus."

"We'll talk about it when I come home," he promised. The train whistle shrieked again. "I have to go."

"Will you get home from Camp Lewis before you're sent across?" She clasped both hands around his arm in a death grip.

"I don't know, but if I don't, I want you to know, I want you to remember something."

Devotion mingled with a strange shyness, a trait others would never have believed in Timothy Wainwright. "I love you."

"I know. I love you too. Ever since Father married your mother and you came to live with us." Some of her worry dwindled. Surely he would remember what she said and her prayers would never be lost.

Timothy towered over her five-feet four-inch frame like a cathedral next to a single-story building. He looked deep into her amber eyes. "That's not what I mean." His hoarse voice and changed face sent a wondering thrill through the girl who adored him.

"I love you as a man loves a woman. Hope, can you, do you think you could ever, learn to care for me — that way? Not as a dear sister but as someone I want for my wife?"

Too stunned to reply, Hope's brain whirled. She stared into the familiar face that somehow looked older and more mature. Did going away to fight for freedom and those left behind do this to young men? What of the cataclysmic feeling inside her that the world could never be the same as it had been just moments ago?

"I'm sorry. I shouldn't have told you," he whispered. He gently freed his arm from her nerveless fingers and managed a crooked smile, his eyes anxious. "Forget what I said —" His face changed. "*No!* I meant every word. Remember, even if you don't hear from me, I love you. There won't be a day or night I don't think of you and I'm coming back." He gripped her hands until they ached. "I'm coming back, Hope, and when I do, Luther Jones or your father or the devil himself won't keep me from asking you to marry me!" He leaned forward, boyishly pressed a kiss on her lips, then caught her close. "Don't forget me."

The next instant he raced toward the already-moving train and swung on the lower step. "Goodbye, my dear."

Hope's blurred vision melted the edges of his trim figure until he became a shape instead of her beloved brother. Her heart pounded under the bodice of the modest blue frock she'd worn because Timothy liked it. She waved a lace-edged handkerchief with one hand and impatiently brushed away tears with the other. "Goodbye. . . ." But when the train rounded a bend and only a smoky trail and dwindling hum remained, her heart added, *Goodbye, my dear.*

"*How dare you behave like a woman of the streets?*"

Instantly Hope spun around. Tall, massive, his haughty face alit with anger, Justin Farrell grabbed his daughter's arm and strode down Main Street toward the finest home in town.

"You're hurting me, Father." Hope tried to free her arm.

His hand tightened until she felt she must cry out with pain. Instead she breathed a prayer for help and brokenly replied, "He had to have someone to see him off. You said you wouldn't come. I'm all he has."

"He has nothing, and that includes you," he raged, keeping his voice down so curious passersby could not hear. "He chose to disobey my wishes —"

"Your *commands*," she substituted with an unusual degree of resistance. "You never asked him not to go. You ordered him."

"*Silence*." Justin's lips thinned. "I will not be the laughingstock of Dale! How could you allow him to hug you, to kiss you in front of half the town?"

Hope's heart sank. She had fervently prayed her father missed some of Timothy's parting. "He's my brother."

Justin's nostrils flared like a runaway horse with the bit between his teeth. "*Step*brother. You didn't look very sisterly to me. I won't have it, do you hear me?"

It would only make things worse to argue. Hope knew from experience the only way to settle her father to the point of reason was to keep quiet, try and ignore the hurtful things he said, and wait until his temper cooled.

His accusations drummed in her ears until Hope wondered if Timothy wouldn't find more peace on the battlefront than she at home. A little shudder ran through her. At least Father hadn't heard Timothy's declaration of love or he would be repeating it and cheapening it into something common and not of the spirit. Gratefulness and a strange wonder at her own reaction helped drown out some of the din around her.

Once inside the cool hall of their home, Justin pointed to the curving staircase. "Go up to your room and stay until you're called for lunch." He leaned against the highly polished newel post. "You might consider my feelings for a change. I have a responsible position. How do you think I'm going to feel when people come into my bank and send sly looks at me because my daughter and —" he paused, choking, "my daughter doesn't even have the decency to protest when the worst young man in town kisses her in public?"

Hope's good intentions to keep quiet were a poor opponent for her savage emotions.

14

"Timothy Wainwright *isn't* the worst man in town! Your precious Luther Jones was the one who did the things the town — and you — blamed on Timothy." A sob escaped. "If you'd ever investigated instead of accusing Tim of lying then swallowing everything Luther told you —"

"Go to your room!"

She fled from the menace in his face, the almost fanatical light in his eyes. She should never have spoken like that. If ever anyone idolized another human being it was her father and his obsession with Luther, the son of an old friend. How could she have so quickly forgotten that in defense of Timothy?

Skirts bunched up from her slippers, Hope ran up the long staircase, down the hall and into her room. Not even the cream-colored wallpaper with its pink and blue nosegays and matching bedspread cheered her. She flung herself on the sturdy sleigh bed and buried her hot face in a hand-embroidered pillowcase.

A confusion of thoughts attacked her weary mind. Why did she feel so strange when Timothy kissed her? The love in her heart had suddenly taken on a new dimension when confronted with her father's unjust accusations. Most of all, Timothy's

15

refusal to accept Jesus because of the long-held bitterness over Luther darted in and out of her mind.

"Please, God, no matter what it takes, bring him to You." Her whisper echoed in the still room. Did she mean that? Could she face whatever Timothy might be required to go through to find salvation? Hope trembled and her mouth went dry. Then the soft chin took on some of her ancestors' sternness. "According to Your will, Lord."

For hours she lay on her bed, staring at the ceiling and out the wide window toward the south and west. How long would it take the train to reach Camp Lewis, south of Tacoma? Would Timothy be settling into his barracks now or standing in line for uniforms? If only she had thought to ask more about what lay ahead. Yet in the few days since he turned twenty-one and announced his intention to join the army, Justin's fury had left no time for questions.

"The hills of Hope," he had teased. She looked at the distant mountains. How remote they seemed, how untouched! Yet scientists said some of them had once been active volcanoes erupting with such force that rocks showered for miles around. She could well believe it. Digging in Dale and the surrounding area meant removing rocks larger than her head.

Hope burned inside at her father's wrath until the welcome numbness on the outside vanished and left her aching. Finally she stumbled out her door to the adjacent bathroom. Ice cold water helped soothe her face and, with another desperate prayer for calmness and strength, Hope changed her gown and prepared to answer the lunch summons. Her chin high, her soul strengthened by prayer, she caught sight of herself in the mirror and gasped. Not a girl but a woman looked back at her with an air of determination and a telltale expression in dark amber eyes that must be carefully guarded.

Timothy's outburst had done this. Already his impetuous confession had altered the affection and comradeship they had known: She believed in him and her attempts to defend him against injustice had been futile at best.

"Miss Hope, lunch is ready." Maura Cullen, red-haired, blue-eyed, and Irish, tapped at the partly open door. "Faith, and are ye all right?" Only Maura's love for Hope and Timothy had kept her on in the Farrell household in spite of Justin's heavy hand.

"Timothy's gone," she whispered.

17

Before her friend could respond, Justin's autocratic voice boomed up the stairs. "Maura, stop gossiping and get lunch on the table. I have to get back to the bank for a meeting. Hope, quit dawdling."

"Yes, Father." *Sometimes it's hard to honor him,* Hope thought, and slowly she descended to the hall level. To her amazement her father said no more concerning Tim or the morning incident. She gradually relaxed and even managed to enjoy Maura's excellent biscuits, ham, applesauce, and salad.

When Justin rose at the end of the meal, Hope timidly said, "I thought I'd walk to the library this afternoon and see Grace Forsythe." She held her breath and wondered if her banishment to her room would extend all day.

"Stop by the bank on your way. I have a paper she asked me to prepare." His dispassionate glance swept over her. "You may as well do something useful."

Hope flushed and opened her lips to protest. It wasn't her fault she didn't have a job in a store or school or even in the bank. She'd asked a dozen times and all she got was the curt reply, "You have plenty to do keeping Maura busy and besides, no daughter of Justin Farrell is going to wipe schoolchildren's noses or measure out flour

18

for a bunch of louts." Until now Hope had given in. The big house needed a lot more time than Maura could give if she worked twelve hours a day. Justin demanded instant readiness in case he invited unexpected guests home for meals or to stay. In spite of the housework burdens Hope volunteered many hours rolling bandages and knitting for the men overseas, all the while wishing she could train as a nurse. If things continued as they were, every able pair of hands would be needed before this horrible war ended.

The one time she broached the subject of training, the ceiling, in the guise of Justin Farrell, came crashing down on her head.

"My daughter wash men's bodies? Never!"

Yet Hope knew in her heart that if the war went on until she turned twenty-one, all her father's protests wouldn't hold her back. Compassion for Timothy filled her. His two years' seniority freed him from his stepfather's tyranny while Hope must wait and make the best she could of a closed or at least stalemated situation.

She breathed an actual sigh of relief when Justin marched out the front door secure in his own importance. She quickly helped Maura clear the table, washed and wiped the lunch dishes while Maura prepared a dinner dessert, and started the vegetables and then reset the table.

"Run along and have a good time," Maura ordered when Hope asked what else needed to be done. "I'll be putting the roast in later and you can pick and arrange fresh flowers when you get back. Didn't I hear himself telling ye to stop by the bank? He won't stand for loitering."

Hope smiled at the way Maura lapsed into her Irish *ye* now and then. All her years in America hadn't erased the faint brogue as much a part of her as her spotless white aprons. Hope impulsively hugged the older woman and the answering smile warmed the very cockles of her heart, as Maura often said. "I'll be back in plenty of time to do the flowers," she promised.

"Get along with ye," Maura scolded, but Hope caught concern in the loch-blue eyes. Living with "himself" meant a life of utter subservience and eternal patience. Hope knew the faithful servant often held her Irish tongue when her temper roused on behalf of the two grown-up children Maura still considered her charges.

2

"Whatsamatter, Tim? Cinder in your eye?"

Tim whirled, irritated at being caught straining his vision for the last wave of a lacy handkerchief before the train swung round a curve. Sam Johnson, a fellow baseball player from high school, lounged on the step above him.

Tim started to make a wise remark but Sam's freckled face and soft brown eyes showed understanding. His freckled hand shot out and gripped Tim's. "She's a swell girl. Wish I had someone like her watching me out of sight."

Filled with the pain of parting, the memory of Hope's lips on his choked off anything he might say.

"I sure am glad you talked me into waiting until you enlisted," Sam eagerly told him. "Maybe we can go all the way together."

"I hope so." Tim followed his long-time friend into a crowded car and called out sallies to a dozen boys and men who greeted him.

"Now boys," one of the Spanish-American veterans facetiously warned. "Don't get any ideas about being a hero. It takes us older and more experienced men to win the pretty ribbons and shiny medals."

A roar of laughter followed and Sam retorted, "Oh, yeah, Grampaw? Well, let me tell you, none of us is going to have time to bring home those ribbons and medals. Once the enemy learns the men of Dale have arrived on foreign soil, I reckon they'll just turn tail and run."

"Hooray for Johnson and the men of Dale!" someone shouted. In the furor Tim joined in the morale-boosting exercise he knew hid the same fear of the unknown everyone bound for Camp Lewis felt, especially the older men who had been in war. Yet wasn't this new conflict far different from what they had faced? For the first time in history, fighting in the air — dogfights — had joined with land and sea battles. Tim hid an involuntary shudder. Airplanes raining destruction from above rang a faint bell in his mind. Didn't the Bible talk about the terrible things that would occur before the world as man knew it ended? Some of his Sunday school lessons must have gone deeper than he realized. Could anything be worse than what lay ahead? For one cowardly moment he wondered why he had been so eager to join up. He could have waited for the draft and perhaps never been called.

He looked from face to face, some anxious, some feigning boredom, others apprehensive or alert. Not all of them would come back; even if they did, some might be maimed or gassed or shellshocked. A vision of the Dale families who had buried their sons rose before him. With a mighty effort he shrugged. Hope and a few others would care if his number came up in France or Germany; Justin Farrell would not.

Tim clenched his hands into fists. Not all the wars were fought overseas. Since his own father died years before, every day had been a battle. To survive on the meager living Mother eked out as a milliner, supplemented by his sporadic earnings from errands, was difficult but later . . .

Tim turned off the past with the ease of long practice. Why waste time reliving unpleasant scenes?

All the way to Camp Lewis the "men of Dale," as Sam dubbed them, traded insults about their shooting ability. A man's skill at hunting often made the difference between enough food in hard times and going without. Even the youngest boys, those who had stretched their actual seventeen years to eighteen on the enlistment forms, were crack shots. Would the army recognize their marksmanship and use it?

"Why don't we just tell them we're to-gether?" Sam's innocent-looking eyes twinkled.

"Not a bad idea," a veteran agreed. "Maybe they'll let us all stay home and train someone else to go do the shooting." A wave of boos greeted him. Yet when they reached Camp Lewis and saw the rigid columns of marching men, the enormous parade grounds, the clean white spire of the military chapel, and the ever-present stars and stripes flying in the breeze, the laughter and joking died.

"We've a job to do and we're gonna do it," a burly uniformed sergeant barked when the men of Dale joined a hundred others for orientation. "It ain't easy and it ain't fun, but it's our job. In the next few weeks I'm gonna run and work you like you've never been run or worked before. I'll tell you this once, then you can put it in your pipes and smoke it. I don't send boys overseas who can't take care of themselves. I send trained men — and God help any of you who think otherwise!"

A mighty cheer broke out and Tim could have sworn he saw the rough sergeant blink.

But the next instant he doubted it.

"Except for you veterans I never saw such a puny bunch of Mama's boys. Every batch they send me's greener." He singled out Sam and pinned him to the ground with a glare. "You, there. Ever shoot a weapon?"

"Yessir." Sam's eyes gleamed and Tim coughed to cover a smile. He and Sam shared honors for the best shots in Dale.

The sergeant's frozen stare shifted to Tim. "What's wrong with you? Got consumption or something?"

"No, sir." Tim straightened and set his lips in a firm line.

The sergeant snorted and turned back to Sam. "Step out here."

Sam obeyed and the sergeant tossed him his rifle and pointed to a target some distance away.

Sam instantly sighted and sent five shots into the target. The sergeant strode to it. A gleam of surprise and pleasure crept into his face but was quickly replaced with his usual stern countenance. "Soldier, one of those shots missed dead center." He drew his bushy eyebrows together. "No room in this outfit for anything except perfection. See that you practice — what's your name?"

"Johnson. Sam Johnson, sir." He handed back the rifle.

"Any of the rest of you know one end of a weapon from the other?"

No one moved a muscle but the sergeant's keen eyes didn't miss a thing. When Tim involuntarily brushed a fly from his cheek the sergeant inquired, "Got a problem?"

"No, sir."

"Let's see you shoot. Can you hit the broad side of a barn?"

Tim's mouth twitched in spite of himself. "I hope so, sir."

"You hope so!" The roar turned to a bellow. The sergeant reloaded his rifle in record time and ordered, "Fire at will."

In rapid succession Tim sent five shots crashing into the target. The sergeant inspected it. His mouth hung open. Four shots had gone into the center so close together a pencil lead wouldn't fit between. The fifth entered a mere half-inch away.

"Your name, soldier?" the sergeant demanded.

"Timothy Wainwright."

"Lucky shooting. See that you keep it up. Troops dismissed!"

"How come you had to go show me up?" Sam complained with a grin. "It took my first shot to get used to his weapon."

A matching grin spread across Tim's face. His eyes glowed. "I noticed that, and allowed for it when I shot!"

"Well, I'll be —" Sam shook his head and laughed until tears fell, but the other men of Dale crowded around their own and slapped them on their backs.

" 'Course like the man said, pretty lucky shooting," the veteran Sam had nicknamed Grampaw drawled. "Wait 'til he gets an eyeful of some real shooting."

For the first time Tim felt accepted by his comrades. Growing up as the town's bad boy, excelling only at sports, he'd often been lonely, especially around the older townspeople. The leaders of Dale naturally sided with Justin Farrell, respected banker and pillar of the church. Although they cheered his ability on the ballfield, when parties occurred in the town's "best" homes, Luther Jones and Hope Farrell were always invited while Timothy Wainwright's name was carefully omitted. Maybe that explained his friendship with Sam: Sam's sturdy farmer parents couldn't have been less in awe of the banker. Their rolling fields and sprawling farmhouse offered more of a real home to Tim than he'd known since his mother married Justin.

True to his promise, Sam Johnson risked censure and boldly sought out the gruff sergeant whose name turned out to be Kincaid.

"Sir, the men of Dale are all crack shots. Is there any chance we can stick together?"

"You'll go where the army tells you," came the curt reply but a thoughtful look crept into the seasoned warrior's face. "I suppose you want to stick with the boys from home too?" he asked Tim.

"Only if that's what my country wants of me. I just want to get over there, get it over with, and come home."

"Don't we all?" Suddenly Sergeant Kincaid seemed almost human. As if to make up for the momentary weakness, he blared, "Don't say anything to anyone about what you want and don't want. And call me sir!"

"Yes, sir!" Tim's ears tingled. How could he have forgotten himself enough to state his views without being asked?

Yet a little later Sergeant Kincaid called the men of Dale together. "We're going to have a little rifle practice." He led them back to the field. One by one the Dale men fired, chalking up an impressive number of direct hits, with no bullets flying wild and few shots near the target edges.

"Enough." Kincaid turned to several high ranking officers who stood nearby observing the demonstration. "Well?"

"Put them in D company — all of them,"

a major ordered. "That is, if you think you can teach them what else they need to know."

Sergeant Kincaid didn't blink an eyelash. "I'll teach them." The grim set of his jaw boded no good for slackers, yet Tim and Sam exchanged delighted grins behind his back, along with their comrades. "D for Dale, Kincaid to aid," irrepressible Sam mouthed.

Tim kept his face straight but a strange happiness, a sense of belonging warmed him. *I'll do my best,* he promised, facing the hills of home. *Even if I don't come back, some of D company, including the men from Dale, will. Maybe one day even Justin Farrell will realize I fought valiantly and the whole town will know their bad boy was worth more than they believed.*

He blinked. Hope needed no reports of heroism; he had been her hero since childhood. Often sullen, sometimes guilty, still she had given him her love and faith.

When he unpacked his suitcase he discovered a small plainly wrapped package with the inscription "Tim" in Hope's handwriting. He opened it with his back to Sam and the others. A small New Testament he had seen Hope carry opened naturally to John 3:16 and to a brief note:

Dearest Tim,

I couldn't let you go without arming you with the only protection I know — the love and mercy of God — and my prayers. Never forget that *Timothy* comes from a Greek word that means "honoring God." Deep in my heart I can't help believing that one day you will accept His Son.

Goodbye until we can be together again.

Your loving sister,
Hope

Tim swallowed hard, buttoned the little book in the left front pocket of his newly received uniform, and turned to join Sam for mess. All through supper he cracked jokes until Sam cocked an eyebrow but kept still. In the August twilight just before taps, Tim wrote a letter. He poured out the events of the endless day, choosing to ignore its beginning until near the end of the letter. He told of the marksmanship demonstration and how he later found the New Testament. After a long hesitation he wrote the following:

. . . so here I am, in the army. No one knows where we'll be sent or when.

There are the inevitable rumors. I know we'll be busy — Sergeant Kincaid has promised that! Maybe after we get our basic training we'll be allowed to come home before shipping out.

I've thought at times how I hated Dale because of the way folks treated me. Now I know that the hills of home — and of Hope — are far dearer than I ever realized.

It's funny, too, but after today's rifle practice and being assigned to company D, which Sam Johnson says stands for the men of Dale, there's a kinship between us that's hard to explain. Perhaps it's because we're all involved in helping to make the world a safe place for wives and sweethearts and sisters. Or the fact we have a job to do and it won't get done without every one of us doing our best. That best may require lives. I pray it won't. But Hope, if something happens and I don't make it back, just remember the one who loves you more than life.

The first plaintive note of taps sounded. Tim hastily scrawled his signature, stuffed the letter in an envelope, and addressed it. With any luck, he'd have an answer within a few days since Dale wasn't all that far from Camp Lewis.

Long after the last ribald comment and the last muffled laugh, Tim lay awake in his bunk. How different it was sleeping in a barracks! At home his small room housed himself and enough furniture to get by. He could lie in bed and count the stars; tall tree branches gently touched his window. He grinned in the darkness. How many times had he slithered through his open window and down the trunk of the enormous fir after being consigned to his room for one of Luther's sins? Strange that Justin had never caught him.

His uneasy contentment fled at the thought of Luther. Lucifer was more like it. Blond and arrogant, from the time he appeared in the Farrell household trouble followed. More than anything else on earth Tim hated a liar, a coward, and a sneak. Luther was all three. He presented a bland expression of wounded innocence when accused of transgressions and his angelic expression invariably won Justin's trust. Sometimes Tim wondered how his stepfather would feel if forced to confront his favorite's wickedness . . . and the countless times he had punished Tim unfairly, even when Hope told him what happened. Would Justin *ever* apologize?

"Some chance," Tim whispered into his

hard pillow and tried to drown out both his angry memories and the snores of his bunkmates. He deliberately switched his thoughts back to Hope, remembering the startled look in her amber eyes when he confessed his feelings. Would he have had the courage to do so if he hadn't been leaving? Perhaps. Ever since he overheard Justin and Luther discussing a possible alliance between Luther and Hope he had nursed the knowledge he'd run away with her and marry her before letting any such wedding take place. Luther, whose name Hope had ruefully told him meant "famous warrior," would trample and destroy Hope. Ironic that Luther with his German ancestry could soon be sent to fight the Huns.

Until early morning Tim's busy brain refused to still and let him sleep. Rest only came when he forced everything out except the snow-capped mountains, green valleys, clear streams, and deep forests of Dale. Home. Hope. Barely conscious, his hand crept to the little book he had placed under his pillow. Somehow it brought him closer to the girl he loved.

A week later Tim dragged in from maneuvers, bone-weary, sweat-stained, and dryer than the Sahara. Sergeant Kincaid's threat to run and work those men was not an idle one. All Tim's experience in climbing, skiing, and baseball got him through but no more. Yet pride in the men of company D kept a grim smile on his face. The harder the tasks set by Kincaid, the more determined the Dale contingent became. They welded into a body of soldiers who never tired of arguing over who could do what best yet fought at the slightest hint of insult by anyone else.

If the future hadn't loomed so dark and uncertain, Tim would have reveled in the training. Yet ever-increasing reports of worsening conditions and casualties leaked back from the front. Prisoners who escaped told of inhumane treatment; wounded military men sang the praises of the Red Cross who labored as close to battle and kept the coffee hot, the morale high. Incredible tales of bravery became the stuff of legend.

A quart of water and a hot shower later, Tim felt more like himself. He stretched on his bunk for the few minutes until mail call. Why hadn't Hope written? It shouldn't have taken this long to get an answer. She must know he would worry until he heard, after taking liberties with her that day at the station. The thought brought him off his bunk and to his feet. He automatically smoothed the tautly drawn blankets in case of a surprise inspection and loped outside. First in line at mail call, he passionately wished he'd been named Allison or Adams or Baker instead of Wainwright.

"Johnson."

Sam's face broke into a grin and he reached for his letter and a package from home.

On and on the names droned until at last the mail clerk called, "Wainwright."

"Here." Tim broke through the ranks of men reading letters from home or still waiting to be called. He accepted the single letter, glanced at it, and froze. *What on earth!* Why would Justin Farrell be writing to him?

Color drained from beneath his bronzed skin as he ripped open the outer envelope. Could Hope be sick? Would even that cause Justin to overcome his dislike enough to inform Tim?

The envelope dropped and Tim sucked in his breath. He stared at a second, smaller letter, the one he had written to Hope that first night at Camp Lewis. It had obviously been opened, but Tim's shocked senses barely registered the rudely torn edges. Instead, they focused on the bold black writing Justin effected, a sign of his power. The words leaping off the paper attacked him like sniper fire:

YOUR BOASTINGS AND
PROTESTATIONS OF LOVE
UNWANTED. FUTURE
COMMUNICATIONS WILL BE
BURNED UNREAD.

Justin Farrell

3

Fury rose in Tim stronger than any emotion he had ever experienced, stronger even than his love for Hope. He shouldered his way through the laughing crowd and headed for the far boundaries of Camp Lewis, blindly trudging, needing to be alone for a fight that had nothing to do with Kaiser Bill.

The branches of a huge fir tree, much like his escape route back home, offered protection and welcome. Without regard for his uniform, he crashed under the interwoven branches and buried his face in his arms. Bad enough for Justin to mock him and accuse him of boasting. But to drag his stepson's love into the open soiled it. "I hate him, God. The hypocrite. Praying openly on Sunday, destroying lives the rest of the week!"

A hundred memories flooded his thoughts. Justin, coldly informing the boy who had hoped for a real father there would be no foolishness in his house. Justin, looking almost pleased at every opportunity to punish the boy for the slightest infraction. Justin, overriding his second wife's rare protests and ordering Hope to her room when she pleaded her adored stepbrother's innocence or begged her father to have mercy.

The boy who remained inside the man under the fir writhed and groaned. If things had been unpleasant the first few years, they became unbearable when he was sixteen.

Tim and Hope had only begun to overcome some of their grief at the death of Tim's mother. Frail and tired, her heart had simply refused to go on. Tim secretly despised Justin for the showy casket and society funeral when he would have liked a simple service with only Hope, Maura, and a few other close friends.

Soon after, an unexplained telegram resulted in Justin's announcement that he had to make a long trip. Tim controlled his face so not to show his joy. The weeks without Justin showed Tim what heaven must be like. He and Hope went to school as usual, and did their chores and lessons. Except for that, the entire Farrell household changed. Maura cooked every delicacy she could concoct, grimly paying for luxuries Justin refused to have her purchase on the grounds they were too dear.

"Himself with all he has," she confided to Tim. "Well, I've a bit saved and we'll have a holiday."

Tim barely caught her words when she muttered, "It'll be the last if what I suspect's true." He tried to question her but Maura shook her red head and clammed up.

A telegram received a month later left the household in an uproar:

HOME NEXT WEEK.
MOVE TIM UPSTAIRS.
PREPARE HIS ROOM.

"Why should Timothy have to move?" Fourteen-year-old Hope demanded. Her amber eyes darkened and flashed. "That old room upstairs is poky." Then horror filled her face. "You don't think Father is bringing home a *wife*, do you? Not right after —" A quick glance at Tim brought a soft cry. "I'm sorry, Tim. Of course that isn't it or he wouldn't want your room made ready."

Tim's boyish mouth relaxed. His first thought had been the same. He shrugged. "I don't really mind. I'll be closer to Maura." Maura's blue Irish eyes misted over.

"That ye will. An' it won't be poky, either." She picked up the gauntlet and the next few days saw Tim's treasures safely toted up the stairs and stashed away, including his mother's picture.

"There." Maura finished straightening the bedspread. "It's small but it's your own." She wiped a tear onto her apron and sighed. "Now to clean the other room."

After she lumbered downstairs Hope stared around the little room. "Do you really like it, Tim?"

He compared the crowded space with the big airy room then looked out the window Hope had polished until it sparkled. From up here he could see almost straight across to the white-capped mountains. The fir tree he knew from his room downstairs also shaded this abode. A little smile erased his scowl. "Yes, I do." He glanced at the door and felt the key in his pocket Maura had given him. Tim never knew why he had sensed the need for privacy. He wouldn't have to let anyone in ever unless he wanted to.

True to his word, Justin was not alone. As he strode up the walk into the hall he was closely followed by a stocky, blond-haired boy of eighteen. Tim disliked him on sight. At everything Luther Jones said, Justin's face lighted up, the way it never had for Timothy. The way Luther boldly stared at Hope through his thick, blond lashes confirmed Tim's impression.

"Luther is your new brother." Justin folded his arms across his massive chest and oozed satisfaction. "He's the son of an old friend. He's been living with an uncle since his father died but this is his home from now on. Since he's older, he will be in charge when I'm not here." His eyes bored into Timothy's but the younger boy didn't betray his apprehension. Somehow he knew the only way to meet Luther's insolence was by indifference.

Until he graduated at eighteen, Tim took the brunt of Luther's abuse — and the punishment for his misdeeds. Time after time Justin whipped Tim when Luther lied until Tim learned not to bother defending himself. Only once in the dead of night had he stalked the wily Luther, pounded him good, and slipped back up his friendly tree to safety. He appeared sound asleep when Justin burst in on him after Luther dragged himself home. His question, "Me? How could I beat Luther up when you sent me to my room hours ago?" established his innocence without a lie.

The day after graduation Timothy approached his stepfather. "Will you lend me money for college?"

"*College!*" Justin's full lips sneered. "You'd be expelled the first month. I've arranged for you to work on a farm in Idaho. You won't get paid but you'll get your board and room."

And be far away from me, his attitude implied.

Tim showed a new conviction. "My mother wanted me to go to college. I intend to do what she wanted."

"We'll see, won't we? Besides, even if I wanted to send you to college — which I don't — I'm not made of money. Luther still has two years to go." Pride lifted the corners of his lips and softened his eyes. "He's going to go far."

Too far, Timothy wanted to add. If Luther's boasts were to be believed, he had hit Harvard like a British tank and was all that held the long-established school together.

"Thank you for your trouble in arranging a job," Tim forced himself to say. "But I won't be needing it." He slipped from the room before Justin could make another scathing comment.

Tim came from a long line of fighters on both sides. If Mother could raise him on her tiny wages, surely her strong, healthy son could achieve her biggest dream and go on to college. He approached every businessman in town for a job and received headshakes from them, even when he knew they needed help. The butcher made no pretense. "Your father's visited us all," he told the irate boy. "Says it's his wish for you to go to Idaho."

"He's not my father," Tim spit between his teeth and moped home, wondering what to do next.

Maura raised her eyebrows when he told her what had happened. "Of course, I can't be for giving advice." Her floury hands stilled on her bread board. "But if I were to be needing a job with himself so important in Dale, I'd find pastures greener away from here."

"Thanks, Maura." Timothy's spirits bounced back up.

"Your blessed mama used to say there's more than one way to skin a cat," Maura reminded, face bland but eyes atwinkle. "And if I've ever taught ye anything it's that the good Lord helps them what help themselves."

Hope helped Tim write letters, lent him money to visit Bellingham Normal School, and secretly supported him with a tear-filled heart. How could she manage without him? Yet she feared the time when Luther would finish his college course and be home for good, taking his place as Justin Farrell's right-hand man in the bank.

"Isn't it funny you want to become a teacher?" Hope laughed one starry evening when she and Tim sat on the front stoop waving to friends and neighbors who strolled by, visiting with those who stopped to chat. "I never thought you liked school very much."

"I liked learning," he said carelessly. "I made up my mind a long time ago that if I ever could teach I'd make lessons interesting." He drew in a deep breath of cool, sweet, summer air. "I also decided I'd never judge a boy according to what I might have heard about him." He viciously stabbed at a dandelion that had dared poke its head up near the porch.

"Are you going to have enough money?" Hope folded her hands on her white muslin dress. "If I had any I'd give it to you but you know Father." She spread her hands helplessly. "What little he gives me for handkerchiefs and sodas wouldn't help much."

An unfamiliar tenderness for his faithful sister welled up inside Tim. "I'll be all right. I heard today the logging companies up by Granite Falls may be taking on help. All you need to be is strong."

"But logging is so dangerous! Tim, isn't there any other way?" Fear underlined every word.

"No, I've asked everywhere. Once school starts I have jobs stoking stoves and working in the kitchen and dining room, but they'll just pay for my tuition and books. I have to work this summer to get a few decent clothes." He turned sullen. "Seems like he could at least give me enough for that."

Choking softly he quickly said, "I'm sorry, Hope. It's just that I *have* to do this."

"I know." A soft little hand crept into his. "You will, too, no matter how hard it is."

After three years of working summers and at school he completed the normally two-year course and obtained a Life Certificate. America had just entered the war in April 1917 and faced a new dilemma.

Strangely enough, Justin and Hope agreed on something concerning Tim. From January on Tim wanted to throw up his college course and enlist. His letters to Hope poured out his feelings that he should be ready if or when the United States got involved.

Justin's smug, "I knew he'd never stick it out!" and Hope's pleading with him not to do any such thing held him to his studies and he finished his course with honors. He would be twenty-one in a few weeks. Still hoping his school record and athletic prowess would soften his stepfather's stance, he listened to Hope.

She reminded him gently, "In spite of everything, he has to be proud. He doesn't know I saw Luther's grades from Harvard." She grinned and her eyes shone. "Slightly above average."

"You'd never know it by the way he talks about him," Tim grunted. "Since he got home and went into the bank you'd think Luther Jones was second in command to God."

"I know." Hope's laughter vanished. "And since Luther wheedled him into using his influence to get him an officer's commission in the service, Father's been almost impossible to live with at home."

"Then why is he so against *my* joining?"

"He wouldn't be if you'd agree to let him get you a commission instead of insisting on going as a regular doughboy." Her lips twisted. "Isn't it strange? The first thing he's ever really wanted to do for you and it's something you can't — or won't — accept."

"Why should a man be given rank he hasn't earned?" Tim shot back. "The draft is more fair. Every man twenty-one to thirty has to register and if your name's drawn, you serve. Luther thinks he's too good to be a foot soldier. He wants to play chief and not be just one of the Indians. Well, I'm not going to be like that. If it will make you happier, or if you think it may please your father, I'll wait until after my birthday when I'd have to register anyway."

Then had come the final argument. Justin called Tim to the library on the night before his birthday. "Everything is taken care of. Timothy, I must admit I didn't think you had it in you to get through college." His voice remained as calm and dispassionate as if he were ticking off good points about a horse he planned to acquire.

"Since you have, I've arranged for your commission, just as I did for Luther. With my influence, there's no need for you to serve as anything except an officer."

For a moment Timothy felt torn. The unexpected olive branch extended in peace appealed to him after the years of fighting with Justin. Couldn't he take the commission, become a good officer who backed his men, and still feel honorable?

While he hesitated, Justin played his last card and made the worst strategic mistake of his life. "If you refuse, you can no longer consider yourself part of my family. If you follow in Luther's footsteps. . . ." He shrugged and a little smile played over his hard-bitten features.

Springing from his chair, the ugly memories of Luther blurring his vision, Tim faced

Justin angrily. "*Never!* I'd rather die!"

Justin's great fist crashed to the desk. "*Then go!* You are no longer my son —"

"I never was." Timothy compressed his lips. "Even when I wanted a father, someone to listen and care."

"*Silence!*" Standing now, Justin's blood-red complexion and heaving shoulders resembled more a tormented bull than a distinguished banker. "The day you enlist is the day you are the same as dead to me."

Tim wanted to hurl a hundred taunts at his bitter opponent. What he couldn't tell the blinded man before him about his precious Luther! Stories of escapades at officers' training had already drifted back, in keeping with the well-covered sins Luther gathered in his younger years.

A sense of defeat filled him. Even if Justin ever believed him — which he wouldn't — it would only increase his hatred of Tim. Without another word Timothy turned on his heel and left.

Days condensed into hours, then minutes, then the chugging train whistled off carrying Tim and the men of Dale to war. . . .

"Hey, buddy, you around here any-where?"

For the second time Sam Johnson's merry call broke Tim's reverie. He considered staying where he was but Sam's keen eyes would spot him. Tim wormed his way back out from under the branches, brushed off some needles, and grinned at Sam. "Pretty good hideout, huh?"

"Not good enough." Sam's famous smile looked like a white wave against his sunburned face. "Anything I need to know?"

"Why not?" Tim shrugged his shoulders but his lips tightened. "Here." He handed the envelope to his friend and straightened his shirt, covertly watching Sam pull out the inner envelope.

"Old man never let her have your letter, I see."

"You know, I got so mad at him, I never even thought of that." Suspicion ate at him. "What makes you say that?"

"Simple." Sam's brown eyes glowed. "I've got sisters and not one of them rips open envelopes like that. They do it kind of daintylike, either with a letter opener or tearing off a little."

"Thanks." Tim took back the mutilated message. "What am I supposed to do now?" He glared at the letter and crumpled it.

"Hold it!" Sam snatched it back. "Don't you have someone you can send it to,

49

someone in Dale you both trust? I'd say mail it in care of my sisters but they talk too much. What about Maura?"

Tim's jaw muscles relaxed but he shook his head and stared across the grounds toward the chapel. "Justin always gets the mail and sorts it. He'd know and it would just make trouble for her and Hope."

"Well, you can't take off for Europe and not let her know where you are," Sam reminded. He thought for a minute. "I just bet Mrs. Forsythe at the library would pass it on and button her lip." His face lit up. "I remember once she saw me tear a page in one of the books. I didn't mean to, I just turned a page too fast. Anyway, I thought she'd yell when I told her. Instead she thanked me for being so honest and got out some stuff and fixed it."

"I don't know her very well." Tim wavered.

"She's all right," Sam endorsed.

Tim glanced at his watch doubtfully. "There's no time to write anything else to Hope."

"You don't need to." The quiet voice steadied Tim. "Just put the whole thing the way it is in another envelope. Address it to Mrs. Forsythe and she'll know what to do."

"It seems cowardly," Tim rebelled.

"Look, Wainwright, Hope Farrell's the same as in prison. Are you going to let her stay there until the war ends?" Sam punched Tim's shoulder. "If you are, I'm going to start writing to Hope myself. She's too good for Luther Jones."

Tim grabbed Sam's arm instantly, not realizing the strength of his grip. *"What do you mean?"*

Sam jerked free and nursed his sore arm. "Sorry. I thought you knew. Everyone else does," he mumbled and looked down.

"Knew what?" Tim's nerves were on edge.

Sam shook his head and pity filled his eyes. "Half of Dale's laying odds that she'll be Mrs. Luther Jones — and soon. If he gets scheduled for an overseas trip, the gossips have it Justin will push for a hurry-up wedding and get them tied before he goes across."

The confirmation of what he'd suspected but wouldn't face left Tim cold. Even the beating August sun couldn't ward off the chill in his bones. "But she loves me, I know she does. She must!"

A heavy hand came down hard on his back and Sam's warning voice issued a death sentence. "Not many can or will stand against Justin Farrell for long. Best thing you can do is to make sure she's engaged to

51

you before you leave Camp Lewis." He warmed to the idea. "A better plan is for you to marry her as soon as you can. We'll get a few days' leave when we finish basic training. If you can convince her it could save a lot of heartache later. I'll help any way I can."

Get engaged? Marry Hope — soon? Tim felt the way he had when he fell from a window and his breath was knocked out of him. "Impossible!"

"Not if you love her and she loves you." Sam's honest face turned red. "The way I see it, once you're hitched there won't be a whole lot Justin can do."

"What if he throws her out?" Tim would not put such an act beyond Justin.

"Wouldn't she be better off even then than if her father somehow made her marry Luther?"

The mention of Luther cut short any answer Tim might make. "Come on, Tim," Sam ordered. "Sergeant Kincaid just loves it when someone's late." Tim followed a few paces behind, his heart many miles, and whistle stops, away.

4

Hope Farrell patted her blond curls into place, reached for her pink parasol that matched her eyelet-trimmed lawn dress, and slowly walked downstairs. Ten empty days had passed since Timothy rode away to Camp Lewis. Ten days of armed truce with Justin's gimlet eyes observing every move she made.

"It seems that after nineteen years he should trust me," she confided to Maura.

"It isn't *you* he doesn't trust," Maura wisely said. "It's that he's afraid his plans will go gang aftly."

Hope couldn't even smile at her faithful friend's expression. "What plans?"

"It's not for me to say." Yet Maura looked as if a little teasing would melt her resistance.

"I don't think I want to know," Hope told her and Maura's eyes moistened. "Sure, and ye'll be hearing from the lad soon."

"Will I?" Hope raised a chin so like her father's stubborn one. "I suppose he's been busy but almost everyone else has heard." Her lips trembled. "He promised to write."

Maura's soap-covered hands quieted. "You don't think —" she clamped her lips shut.

Hope's eyes widened. "You mean Father may have intercepted a letter?" Fear drained her face of color and for a moment she thought she might faint. *Dear God, what if Timothy spoke of his changed love and Father read the letter?*

"I should be whipped for even hinting such a thing," Maura admonished herself and wiped a drop from her cheek, leaving a streak of suds in its place.

The telephone interrupted their conversation. Maura quickly wiped her hands on a dishcloth and picked up the receiver. "Mrs. Forsythe would like to speak with you."

Hope swallowed her agitation and managed a small, "Hello?"

"Hope." Grace Forsythe's voice matched her personality — brisk, decisive, yet warm. "Something rather unusual has happened. Could you join me for tea about four? I'll close the library half an hour early."

"Why, yes."

"Good. I'll look forward to it."

Hope slowly hung up the receiver. "I can't imagine what is important enough for

Grace to close the library early! She's never done that as far as I know."

"I'll finish up here. Don't be for hurrying. Himself ordered dinner for seven so there's plenty of time."

Hope began her walk down Main Street to the small but charming cottage adjacent to the Dale library where Grace Forsythe had lived for as long as Hope could remember. One of her earliest recollections was of her own mother taking her to visit Mrs. Forsythe, the widow who quickly became "Aunt Grace" to Hope except when on duty in the library. After Hope's mother died, she joined with Maura in giving the child a strong faith in her Lord and a love of books.

Heat shimmered from the storefronts. Flags hung limp from lamp posts and porch overhangs. Hope unfurled her parasol but even its shade offered little relief. A multitude of odors assailed her: fresh-baked goods in the tiny town bakery; dust; the sweet smell of candy and perfume from the drugstore that also served as a confectionery and soda fountain; a sharp tang from the stable; and overripe bananas and aged cheese from the town's largest grocery store. Snatches from "Nola" floated down from an upstairs window, breaking off when fingers hit the wrong piano keys, then continuing with the right melody. The milk delivery wagon rattled past, cans empty. The driver waved and called, "Afternoon, Miss Hope." His leathery face broke into a smile and he reined in his horse.

"Why are you driving?" she asked. "I thought your son always delivered our milk. Is he sick?"

"Oh, no!" The man shook his head emphatically. "He's gone to help fight for our country. Went the same day as Sam Johnson. You remember. Your brother Timothy was in that batch."

Little flags waved in Hope's cheeks. "Oh yes, I remember." She sighed.

"I hope they come back soon." The driver proudly raised his head and Hope followed his gaze to the flag flying over the post office.

"I do, too, Mr. Wilson. It's hard to wait." She glanced down to hide the tears that crept into her eyes.

"My boy Tad says that now company D's got the men of Dale, once they get across they'll show old Kaiser Bill a few things. Well, I better get on home. Lots to do around the place with Tad gone." He clucked to the old white horse who had pulled the milk wagon for years. "Nice talkin' to you."

"Goodbye, Mr. Wilson." On impulse she called after him, "I'll — I'll pray for Tad."

"Mighty nice of you." His face split into another wide grin. "Tad will be glad to hear that too. I'll have Ma tell him when she writes. Giddap." He clanked away down the street.

For some reason, everything felt different today. She'd walked this street a thousand times yet something in the late August air reached out to claim her. A feeling of love for her town and the people filled her . . . if only Timothy could have been given a chance so he could feel this way. Instead, he cherished the surroundings but disdained the townsfolk under Justin Farrell's thumb.

Yet how could it be different? The bank held mortgages on many homes and businesses and her father's fanatic insistence on payments being made on time — regardless of circumstances — forced those dependent on his good will to refrain from crossing him.

Hope loitered in front of a dress shop, admiring the up-to-the-minute styles. Miss Hattie might be getting on in years but she studied *Ladies' Home Journal* and every other magazine or newspaper she could find that showed prevailing styles. She faithfully reproduced copies to keep Dale women fashionable and proud of it. Miss Hattie made most of Hope's gowns but Justin insisted on the finest garments Seattle stores had to offer when it came to party frocks. Today a pale yellow sprigged with tiny lavender flowers with a frill setting off the modest neckline caught Hope's eye. Perhaps Father would allow her to purchase it for the concert in the park. He liked to have her dress "as befitting her station."

The door to Aunt Grace's vine-covered cottage stood open. Hope tapped, called "Yoo hoo," and opened the screen door. The small living room welcomed her but no one appeared. "Aunt Grace?" Hope spied a note on the table.

"Be right back," Grace had written. "I didn't realize I could use more sugar and the grocery boy has already delivered."

Hope sank into a comfortable chair and glanced around. Her gaze rested on the mantel where Aunt Grace kept curious bits of glassware. Today a letter stood propped against a prancing crystal horse. Hope gasped. That looked like Timothy's writing! Disappointment filled her; her heartbeat quickened. Why would Timothy write to Aunt Grace and not to her? Was he sorry for what he said? Had he thought things over and wished he'd remained silent?

"I'm home," a cheery voice called from the kitchen. The slam of the icebox door preceded quick footsteps then Grace Forsythe stood smiling in the doorway. Tendrils of curly white hair had escaped her efficient chignon to frame a roseleaf-shaped face with still-young blue eyes.

"Aunt Grace, why did Timothy write to you?" Hope blurted it out, too shaken to be polite. Her fingers curled into her palms and she held her breath.

"He didn't, Hope. That's why I asked you to come."

"But-but —" Hope turned back to the letter on the mantel.

Grace shook her head. "The letter is yours." She crossed to the mantel and handed Hope the letter. "I'll make our tea while you read it."

Hope never knew when her friend glided out of the room. With a curious sense of foreboding she removed the outside envelope addressed to Mrs. Forsythe. The bold black message in her father's handwriting leaped out at her.

"How could he?" Her wounded cry brought Grace from the kitchen. She barely heard the older woman ask if she were all right. Strong fingers snatched away the rudely torn second envelope and exposed

Tim's firmly addressed letter to her. With a joyous cry she held it to her breast before opening it.

"I didn't read Tim's letter," Grace quietly told her. "Just the outside of the envelope where your father wrote. Read your message, child, then we'll have tea." She disappeared again, leaving Hope to remove her first love letter and savor it in privacy. No, not privacy. When Hope read Tim's words of love the glowering presence of her father reading over her shoulder left her sick and shaken.

Gradually she calmed and when Grace brought in the tea tray with thinly sliced cucumber sandwiches and tiny cakes, she could speak rationally in spite of the hurt and anger in her heart.

"I don't know if I can ever forgive him," she told Grace. "It's cruel and unbearable that Timothy received this blow just when he's having to face war." Her hand shook and the delicate porcelain cup rattled in its saucer. A spurt of anger was rekindled. "How dare he? I am nineteen years old."

"As long as you live in his house, you are subject to Justin's rules," Aunt Grace soberly reminded the distraught girl. Not a trace of a twinkle remained in her blue eyes, only anxiety for the girl she loved as the daughter she never had.

"Then I won't live there," Hope burst out. "I'll find work and live in a boardinghouse or do anything, but I can't stay home if Father cuts me off from Timothy."

"You care that much?"

Something stirred inside Hope, a knowledge that had been growing since that fateful day at the station. Now when her future lay threatened, love opened into full bloom until it left no room in her heart for anything else but God. "Yes," she whispered.

"As Timothy's sister?" Grace probed.

"No, as Timothy's wife — someday, if God brings him safely home." Her face blanched and she threw herself onto her knees by Grace's chair. "What am I going to do? God tells His children to honor their fathers and mothers, but how can I obey Father's orders when it means giving up Tim? I can't and I won't."

For a long time Grace's strong hand stroked the golden curls half-buried in her lap. "We're also told that when we love someone enough to put our lives in their keeping, we will forsake father and mother and cleave unto our mates and become one. Is this the kind of love you have for Timothy?"

"It is." Hope's heaving shoulders seemed

to steady. "It's holy and sacred, and —"

"Hope, is Timothy a believer?"

She shrank from the question. "I know, I pray that he will be."

The stroking hand stilled. Aunt Grace's grave voice reminded, "We are commanded not to be unequally yoked. If you and Timothy don't share a love of and commitment to the Lord Jesus, you'll miss out on much of the happiness that true marriage can bring."

Hope felt like a wishbone. On one side lay the look in Tim's eyes and the new wisdom that had come to her when she read his letter. On the other, the chasm between them yawned wide and accusing: not her father's attitude but their beliefs about God. Could a bridge ever be built? If not, did she dare marry Tim? A house or love built on sand had little chance of surviving.

"If things get too bad you can come to me," Aunt Grace promised.

"Father wouldn't stand for it." The familiar numbness of acquiescence trained into her since childhood crept over Hope. "Besides, would even *you* dare go against Dale's leading citizen?" Scorn left a bitter taste in the girl's mouth.

"Justin Farrell has no hold on me. My cottage is free and clear and mine to do with as

I wish. Mr. Forsythe left me well provided for."

"And your job at the library? Couldn't the town fathers remove you from your post?"

"Landsakes, no, child." Grace's white eyebrows rose and met the soft wave of hair over her forehead. "Who do you think started the library and keeps it financed?"

"*You?*" Hope couldn't believe her ears. "I-I thought the town or Father or —"

"That's what a lot of folks think but they're wrong," Grace said crisply. "My husband arranged it all in the year when he knew he'd be taken soon. He invested wisely." A gamin grin lit up her face. "I wouldn't be surprised if I had more money salted away than anyone in town, including Justin Farrell." She laughed outright at the expression on Hope's face. "Just because I don't live in a mansion or trot around the world or patronize Seattle's shops, people don't recognize it. It's just as well. I'd rather be liked for what I am than what I have." She grew serious. "Don't you see, child, that's what's mostly wrong with your father. He's suspicious that he won't be liked for himself so he has to demand recognition of what he has."

Hope brushed aside Grace's explanation. A dozen ideas chased around in her suddenly fertile brain. "Did you really mean it, about my living here?"

"I did." No compromise touched Grace's affirmation. "I don't suggest that you move out immediately but when things get too much, my spare bedroom's yours for as long as you want or need it."

Relief flooded through Hope and she stopped twisting her handkerchief into knots. Just knowing she had a haven helped. "Isn't it wrong of me to write to Tim when I know how Father feels?" she asked.

"No father has the right to go too far." Aunt Grace set her lips in a straight line. "Child, you should have received this letter over a week ago. How do you think Tim felt waiting for an answer? How do you think he feels now, wondering what you're going to do? Sit down and write to him." She pointed to a well-stocked desk. "Take as long as you like. Tell him to send your letters to me and that I guarantee no one will see what he writes — even me."

For a long time after Aunt Grace took the tea tray to the kitchen Hope stared at a sheet of blank paper faintly scented with some dried flower petals kept in the stationery drawer. She could hear the clink of silver and dishes as Grace washed, dried, and put away the tea things. Finally she dipped the pen in ink and began writing. Hesitantly at first, she explained she had only received his letter a little while before; then more rapidly she poured out her anger and shock. The only thing she could not bear to include was the realization of how her love had changed from sisterly to something far deeper. Aunt Grace's warning about being unequally yoked together had gone deep. As a child of God, did she even have the right to consider linking her life with someone who didn't know and serve Him?

Tim's statement, *I can't see that God has ever done anything for me,* set an effective check on her pen and her desire to confess her own love. She contented herself with saying, "I long for you to come home on leave. There is so much to discuss." She signed it, "Your loving Hope," and stuffed it in an envelope. She found a stamp, sealed and addressed her letter, and went to the kitchen.

"I'm going to stop and get this mailed so it will go out first thing in the morning."

"Good." Grace walked with her to the door. "Remember, any time you need a place to stay, I'm here."

"You almost sound as if you know that time is coming soon. Why, Aunt Grace?" She peered into the unsmiling face.

65

Grace Forsythe never minced words. "You might as well know. The rest of the town already does. Your father's biggest dream is to see you marry Luther Jones."

A ripple of laughter escaped Hope and she leaned against the door frame for support. "Marry *Luther?* Not if he were the last unmarried man in the state of Washington." She shuddered and wiped her mouth with her crumpled handkerchief. "He tried to kiss me last time he was home. Ugh! He's repulsive."

Grace patted her shoulder. "If you can keep your father — and Luther — from knowing how you feel about Timothy, it's for the best. Timothy's never had anything Luther didn't covet, including his reputation in town. Walk softly, Hope, and keep very close to your Heavenly Father. Not all the battles ahead are overseas." She sighed and Hope's keen ears caught her concern.

5

Before Hope could get a reply to her hastily written letter, Luther Jones arrived in Dale. Justin Farrell did everything except hire a band and roll out a velvet carpet. He arranged a reception and, in a rare magnanimous mood, invited the entire town of Dale to help celebrate Luther's newly acquired officer status. For the first time in years the double doors of the great parlor were thrown open. Justin hired day help to assist Maura and Hope in a cleaning that made military regulations look sloppy. He even went to Seattle and found the best small orchestra to play at the gala event.

The only thing Hope found good about the ostentatious display was his abhorrence of dancing. The idea of having Luther's arms around her made her cringe. At least she'd be spared that.

If she had doubted the importance of the occasion, her father's attitude about her gown settled it. He accompanied her to the most exclusive modiste in Seattle; Miss Hattie's or one of the big Seattle department stores would not be adequate this time. Women who were self-employed as modistes — makers of or dealers in fashionable apparel — were renowned for their one of a kind creations.

Bolt after shining bolt brought a negative headshake until Justin's gaze rested on a shimmering white silk. He lifted the fabric and grunted approval. "This, I think." He contemptuously shoved aside a dozen dainty laces and reached for a handmade cobwebby lace that looked like spun moonlight. "Inset in the skirt," he ordered. "Like the model."

A little warning bell rang in Hope's brain. "But Father, that's a wedding dress! The style isn't at all suitable for a reception."

"It will serve the purpose beautifully," he blandly said and gave the modiste a wintry smile. "It will be extra money in your pocket if you let other things go and make this dress immediately."

"Oui, monsieur." The petite woman beamed. Hope could almost see dollar signs in her eyes. "You understand, the cost of this frock will be —" she shrugged and named an exorbitant figure.

Justin Farrell didn't flinch. "Of course. A

man in my station knows he must pay for quality, madame." He ushered Hope out, sensing her outrage at such extravagance.

"It's ridiculous to pay that much for any gown! Miss Hattie could have made the same thing for half the cost."

A curious smile and a glow in her father's eyes sent another warning signal through Hope. "The cost is nothing compared with the end result."

Hope didn't dare ask him to explain. But when he took her back for a final fitting she thought, *I wonder what Timothy would say.* A rare look of approval crossed Justin's face.

"You look like your mother did on our wedding day."

Hope remembered how Aunt Grace said he wanted to be accepted and her voice softened. "Thank you, Father."

The next instant he reverted to his usual cold self. "Very nice, madame. Have it finished by morning and I will call for it myself. The gown is for a truly special occasion."

Hope didn't want to go to the station with her father when Luther came but she knew better than to voice her objections. She did refuse to dress up any more than she did most afternoons. Justin eyed her simple middy blouse and white skirt with disfavor. "Why didn't you wear your pink? Or that new yellow you insisted on having?" He pulled a gold pocket watch out and frowned. "Too late now. Well, at least you'll outshine every other girl in town at the reception." He visibly swelled with pride.

Hope didn't reply. *I wish Luther Jones were in China,* she rebelliously thought. The closer to the station they came, the faster Justin walked and the slower Hope's pace became. "Don't dawdle!" He gripped her arm and forced her to hurry. "Do you think I want Luther to arrive and not have his family waiting?"

Hope almost retorted, *He's not our family, Timothy is,* but bit her lip. Why start an argument here and now?

They reached the station with ten minutes to spare. To Justin's satisfaction and Hope's amazement, most of the town and all the eligible young women had turned out. Dainty mulls, dotted Swiss, muslins, silk, real and artificial, linens, and crisp cottons were visible in a rainbow of hues. Hope wanted to laugh. She hadn't seen such an array since the Fourth of July!

"I hope Luther falls in love with one of these girls," she muttered, making sure no one could hear.

"She's a-comin'!" A small boy in knee breeches and flying shirttails had flung himself to the ground and put a carefully scrubbed ear to the tracks. Someone grabbed him back and when the train whistle shrieked and the engineer brought his locomotive to a halt, a cheer broke out.

Luther Jones, resplendent in a tailormade uniform that fitted every contour of his strong body, swung down. A little gasp went through the crowd then someone started, "For He's a Jolly Good Fellow." Hope recognized the voice as belonging to her father's head cashier. Her lip curled and Maura's oft-repeated comment that fine feathers didn't always mean fine birds sent a little smile to her lips.

"Father! Hope!" Satisfaction filled Luther's handsome face. He shook hands with Justin and seized Hope. "How about a kiss for your returning soldier?" His powerful arms went around her and he bent his head, ignoring the scandalous whispers of the crowd.

Hope forced herself not to struggle but turned her head and his hot lips fell on her cheek. Bitterness coursed through her. Justin had been furious when Timothy kissed her in public. Now he stood there beaming and smiling with approval. Aunt Grace's warning about his plans lent strength to Hope and she slipped from Luther's grasp in a burst of renewed dislike. She somehow managed to say, "You're looking well, Luther. Will you be home long?"

"Long enough." A hidden meaning in his triumphant answer spurred Hope to action. She quickly looked past him to the few other passengers alighting from the train. "Oh, there's Theodore Greene. I must speak to him. Theo!" Her slender white figure eluded Luther's grasp. For several minutes she inquired of the dazzled Tad how things were going with the young enlistee who had gone some weeks earlier.

The curious crowd who had gathered more to see the Farrells than Luther melted away. Theodore's parents smiled at Hope and said they'd see her at the reception that evening.

"What's the little old idea of being so unfriendly?" Luther demanded as soon as the Greenes were out of earshot.

"Was I unfriendly?" Hope's amber eyes remained clear and she laughed. "It's not like we're engaged or anything, Luther. You're my brother."

Silenced for the moment, he contented himself with directing all his conversation toward Justin during their walk home. Hope took heart when several pretty girls crowded around and Luther's attention turned to them. Any feeling of escape, however, vanished when she caught a biding-my-time look in Luther's eyes.

"Father, may I see you in the library? Privately?" Luther inquired when they stepped into the cool, spotless hall.

"Of course." The most genuine smile Hope had seen on Justin's face made him seem like the father she had once adored. Uneasily she wandered into the kitchen where Maura worked putting the finishing touches on an early supper. The lavish buffet would be catered but Justin wanted all signs of the supper meal removed before guests started to arrive in a few hours.

"Well?" Anxiety brightened Maura's eyes.

"He hasn't changed. He kissed me in front of everyone. I turned my head, but what if someone writes and tells Tim?" There, she'd said it, the thing that bothered her even more than Luther's rude embrace.

"Tell him first." Maura knew all about the letter Hope had received days late. "Write a note and I'll send a neighbor boy to the post office." She sighed and twitched an apron string that threatened to come undone. "He knows ye and he's for knowing Luther."

"Thank you, Maura." Hope's slim arms slid around her friend's waist then she dashed out and upstairs. With luck, she could just get her letter written while Justin and Luther talked. A steady rumble told her the conversation hadn't ended.

"This is the happiest day of my life," Luther announced over supper. He helped himself to another beaten biscuit, honey in the comb, and sweet butter.

"I didn't know you liked Dale that well," Hope said. Anything to keep him from getting personal. "What was officers' training like? Do you know where you'll be sent?" If her heart added a wish that it would be far away her bright smile hid it.

Luther finished the biscuit and reached for another. "I don't like Dale, especially after four years at Harvard. Of course, it has some compensations." He shot a conspiratorial glance at Justin who actually laughed out loud. "Training? Tough but there are ways to get out of the worst of things." He launched into a series of slightly risqué stories that even Hope knew would have seen him dismissed from training. She hid her disgust at his exaggerations and fixed a smile on her lips.

"Any more pie?" Luther's brusque demand was a poor compliment of Maura's warm apple pie smothered in whipped cream.

"Plenty in the kitchen."

"Bring me another piece!" He didn't even wait for her to get out of the room before he remarked, "Why don't you get rid of her and get someone a little more respectful? She never did like me."

For once Justin didn't agree. "Maura's the best cook in Dale. Her likes and dislikes are her own business." He turned to Hope. "Is your gown pressed and ready?"

"Yes, Father." Hope toyed with her own pie, too annoyed to enjoy it.

"Hope looks just like a bride in her new dress." Justin's eyes gleamed.

Luther choked and then roared with laughter. "Like a bride, huh? I can't wait to see her all decked out in my honor."

"If you'll excuse me, I'll start getting ready." Hope couldn't stay at the table one more minute without bursting into angry tears or telling Luther Jones how she despised him. She rose, nodded to her father, and made her escape.

Luther's voice followed her. "Wonder how she'll take it?"

Take what? Hope hesitated on the staircase. Her veins turned to ice when she heard Justin's warning.

"Shhh. If she finds out now she may fuss. Once she's yours you can handle her and it will be too late."

75

Luther's satisfied laugh freed her from her immobility and she lightly ran upstairs but motioned to Maura, who had come into the hall. Never had the buxom Irishwoman moved so quietly. When they were safe in Hope's pretty room she breathed hard but whispered, "What is it?"

Her face paler than her middy blouse, Hope whispered back, "They're up to something. I'm not sure what." Horror filled her. "You don't think Father has promised me to Luther, do you?" She hastily repeated what she had overheard.

"I wouldn't put it past him." Maura straightened to full height. "Just be for re-membering, he can't force you to do any-thing you don't want. Trust your Heavenly Father and He will open a way for you. The spalpeen! Thinking he can come riding home in a uniform and everyone has to bow down and worship."

"I wish Timothy were here." Hope's legs gave way and she sank to her billowy bed. The current of air from her sudden move-ment rustled the gorgeous white creation waiting to be donned.

"Be glad he's not," Maura wisely told her and stroked the disheveled golden head. "It could be a terrible scene."

"Nothing could be worse than knowing

your own father is conniving with that — that — Luther!" Suddenly a dangerous look overtook Hope's face and she sprang up. "Well, I can play my own game." She hugged Maura until she gasped. "Go back downstairs. Tell them anything you like or nothing. They think I'm getting ready and I am."

The instant the door closed behind Maura, Hope fell to her knees beside her bed and poured out her heart in prayer as she had done so many times before. Gently and slowly peace returned and the feeling God had armed her against whatever lay ahead.

At last she faced the girl in the mirror, almost unable to believe what she saw. The modiste had surpassed herself. Row after row of costly inset lace highlighted the yards of white silk that shimmered with every flicker of light. The gown clung to her slender figure, barely rounded at the neck and billowing at the bottom. If only Timothy . . . but she refused to consider that thought. Her wits must be clean and unclouded by her own feelings if she were to overcome whatever plot had been formed against her.

Something leaped into Luther's eyes — was it admiration, possessiveness? — when she regally descended the curving staircase to greet the first of the guests. Now her training as a Farrell served her well. She held out one white-gloved hand, suffered Luther to take it, and walked with him to the background of glowing red roses her father had ordered erected. Yet what sustained her far beyond her background was the knowledge that as a child of God she could silently call on her Heavenly Father for strength to get through this horrible evening.

Hope chatted with each guest personally, somehow avoiding Luther. At first he didn't seem to mind. A hero's welcome, especially by a bevy of female admirers, fed his vanity. Hope gradually relaxed and in her own natural way made everyone from Justin's business associates to the Greenes and Johnsons feel at home. Little cries of delight greeted the well-laid buffet. Hope barely touched the variety of foods offered as she counted off the minutes until the reception ended and she could escape to her room.

Just when she congratulated herself on her success, a heavy hand fell to one silk-clad shoulder. Another hand under her elbow boosted her to her feet and Justin Farrell tapped on his crystal water goblet for attention. An air of expectancy filled the great room. "It gives me great pleasure to announce the engagement of my daughter Hope," her father's voice boomed. He turned to Luther, placed Hope's nerveless hand in his, and continued. "In keeping with the times, the gown Hope is wearing will also be her wedding dress. If you will assemble yourselves facing the background of roses where we welcomed you, we'll get on with the ceremony."

He actually laughed when the crowd gaped and looked toward Hope. "Things have been arranged for some time. Ah, good. I see Reverend Slater is ready and waiting. Come, Hope, Luther."

It couldn't be happening, but it is, Hope thought wildly. *If I don't speak, I'll be Mrs. Luther Jones, just as Father boasted and the town laid bets. God, help me.*

The memory of a cool morning, the look in a boy-turned-man's eyes and his promise, "I'm coming back, Hope, and when I do, Luther Jones or your father or the devil himself won't keep me from asking you to marry me," sustained her. Tim's words were ringing in her ears: "I love you as a man loves his mate. Hope, can you, do you think you can ever learn to care for me — that way? Not as a dear sister but as someone I want for my wife?"

Was the girl Timothy worshiped so spirit-less she couldn't speak up? *Never!*

Hope pulled her hand free, clapped both hands together, and laughed. Tears of mirth poured down her face.

"Oh, Father, Luther, you're such jokers! You had everyone here actually believing your little announcement." She hurried over to Reverend Slater whose mild eyes looked round with astonishment. "Why, you even helped, didn't you? The perfect touch of au-thenticity." Her laughter rang out again in the stunned silence. "If I hadn't known better, you could almost have fooled me. To think I never knew a thing about it — how could you keep such an exciting joke a se-cret? You must have been planning for some time, just as you said." She made her eyes twinkle then swept her gaze over the horde of guests. "Well, now that the joke's over, how about some music? Aunt Grace, let's start with 'Keep the Home Fires Burning,' all right?"

Grace Forsythe calmly walked to the grand piano, opened and dusted for the re-ception. Her blue eyes sparkled and her commanding voice suggested, "Why not gather close, everyone? Let's blend our voices and see if we can make the popula-tion of Dale that isn't here — which means cats and dogs — hear how we sing." She struck the opening notes. Hope pushed to the front and stood as close to the piano stool as possible. The ranks closed behind her and shut out Luther and Justin, but not for long.

"Now we'll —" Luther began, face like a thundercloud.

"Right. We'll sing for you and all our brave Dale men," Grace said quietly and Luther had to join in the song. As soon as they finished one song, Grace or Hope suggested another. "Roses of Picardy," "Long, Long Trail," and "It's Tulip Time in Holland" were followed by a dozen others more rollicking or poignant. As the clock struck twelve, Grace played the beginning of "God Be With You 'til We Meet Again" and followed it with "The Star-Spangled Banner." After an emotion-filled moment, Hope said, "Thank you all for coming," and guests swept toward the front door, murmuring appreciation and congratulating Justin and Luther on the best joke anyone in Dale had ever thought up.

Aunt Grace engaged the two sullen men in conversation for a moment while the last of the guests disappeared. Hope caught the delicate white folds of silk around her and stole upstairs undetected. Door locked, she tore off the hateful gown and left it in a pile on the floor. Humiliation and gratitude to God warred within her and her revulsion of Luther rose to new heights.

What seemed an eternity later, a knock thundered at her door. Someone turned the knob. Hope's keen ears caught a muttered curse. "She's locked herself in," Luther yelled.

"Keep your voice down. That meddling Forsythe woman is still just outside," Justin said. "Hope, open this door at once."

The knob rattled but the lock held. Surely Father wouldn't break down the door! Hope held her breath and didn't answer.

"Thinks she's smart." Even through the door she could hear Luther's heavy breathing. "She won't get away with it."

Opposition always brought out the worst in Luther and her bedroom door was a simple obstacle in his way. "You were so sure it would work. What's wrong with her? Any other girl here tonight would have gone through with it."

"She and Timothy have taken a fancy to each other," Justin stormed. "But don't worry. She'll forget him and marry you. She's my daughter and by all that's holy she'll do what I say!"

6

When Timothy received the letter Hope wrote at Grace Forsythe's, the gray Camp Lewis skies turned rosy. *She cared.* It showed in every line of her letter. He longed to fall out of marching formation and answer the letter immediately but fate decreed otherwise. Just as he settled down that evening to write, Sam Johnson burst in. "Night maneuvers coming up. Get ready, everyone. Sergeant Kincaid's on his way over."

Company D came alive, showing little trace of the grueling day they had already put in. Grampaw complained, "How do you always know everything, sprout?"

Sam just grinned. "I have big ears."

"Ten-shun!" Sergeant Kincaid appeared in the doorway. "Now we're goin' to find out if you sharp-shootin' galoots are worth anything at night." He grimly waited for the men to struggle into their gear. "It ain't gonna be no Sunday school picnic either."

As usual the sergeant's prophecy came

true. Even the intrepid men of Dale were glad to hit their hard bunks and snatch a little sleep in the few hours before dawn. Timothy's joy proved to be no match for fatigue. Yet every man in company D slept with the sweet knowledge of having done his best.

Another complete day of marching, combat, and firing practice passed before Tim could even think of writing to Hope. When a free hour presented itself after evening mess call he found himself a little shy. Yet the idea the irrepressible Sam Johnson had planted about getting engaged, or better, marrying Hope before he went overseas, had already begun to grow. From considering it ridiculous and impossible, it gradually became an uneasy reality.

Tim forced himself to write of the training, to include funny things Sam and Grampaw and the others said and carefully omit the rougher side, the grim reminder that every maneuver had been geared to turn farmers and boys into fighting machines. The setting sun warned him to hurry and finish to get the letter mailed. Tim took a deep breath and plunged right in.

"I hope you have thought about all I said that last day and in my letter. Hope, will you marry me? Do you love me enough — not as a sister, but to be my wife?"

Before he could reconsider, his heart pounding at his audacity, he stuffed the letter in an envelope, addressed and stamped it, and got it in the mail.

The next few days found Tim too busy to worry over what he had written. Something new had crept into the air. Sergeant Kincaid drilled his men unmercifully and kept pace with the best of them. Rumor had it that when company D shipped out the sergeant would go with them. When big-ears Sam whispered the news, the men of Dale cheered. Although at times they hated the tough sergeant, they respected him for that very quality!

"A good man to have with us," Grampaw summed him up. "If we get in a tight spot Kincaid will be right there with us and not conveniently away from the danger, like some officers I've known."

Before Tim could get an answer to his second letter, he received the short note Hope had written the afternoon Luther arrived home in Dale and then a longer letter telling all about the reception and what had been schemed to be her wedding day. Tim's face darkened and his fury rose, but as he read on, he let loose a blood-curdling war whoop. "Hey, Sam, listen to this!" He went back and read the account of the wedding fiasco.

Sam rolled on the grass. He laughed so hard that even Tim joined him, doubling over in hysterics. However, inside Tim exulted at Hope's quick thinking and her putting Luther and Justin in a position where they couldn't do a thing about the wedding without exposing the whole plot and knowing the whole town despised them.

"More reason than ever for you to marry her," Sam warned when he could talk again. "I wouldn't trust that stepfather of yours any farther than I could throw our bull Old Red. As for Luther Jones —" He raised his eyebrows. "He isn't worth spit."

"I never knew you hated him that much." Tim's dark eyes opened wide. "Most of Dale thinks he's one of God's gifts."

"No, sir! Most of Dale knows he's a skunk. They don't dare say so because your old man owns the town." Sam looked wise and his freckles stood out like rust spots on a tin pail.

"Remember, when we go home, and —" He leaned close and whispered. "If what I hear's true, it won't be long. A few days off then back here to wait for overseas orders. Anyway, whatever I can do to help, just holler."

"Thanks, buddy." His gaze met Sam's

steady look. "It will all depend on Hope." At that moment he realized he had accepted Sam's suggestion. He'd do anything on earth to marry Hope before being shipped out. Not just because he loved her more than life, but to protect her from Luther Jones — and from her father.

Finally the longed-for letter came. The small white envelope looked dainty against Tim's deeply bronzed hand. A single sheet conveyed words that brought a rush of color to the anxious young soldier's face.

Dear Tim,
   I love you in the right way but we'll talk when you come.

                     Hope

If she loved him, Tim pondered, *why didn't she say she'd marry him?* He pulled his brows together then laughed at himself. The important thing was having won her love. Time enough when he reached Dale to decide other things. He was spared the task of not quite knowing what to say when Sam grinned his way into the barracks, bowed low, and stepped aside to let Sergeant Kincaid in.

"Presenting our own Sergeant Kincaid," Sam bowed again.

"Knock it off, Johnson," Kincaid barked but a muscle twitched at the corner of his mouth. He fixed a steely gaze on the men of Dale and said sourly, "In case any of you haven't already been informed by Johnson, the powers that be have decided you need a wet nurse when you go overseas. I get the job."

An involuntary cheer broke out but the sergeant only looked sterner. "That's the bad news. The good news is you can all go home for a few days first." Before anyone could respond he added fiercely, "And if any man's son is one minute late getting back he'll answer to me. Dismissed." He snapped a salute, turned on one heel, and strode out, leaving his men to grin and rejoice.

"About time we saw some action," Grampaw growled and unsuccessfully tried to cover his pride in the boys and men from home. "Now, boys, when we get over there, you just listen to me and we'll be all right." He executed a few ridiculous dancing steps and said in a high falsetto, "We've just gotta show our loving sergeant what good little boys we are. Don't forget your clean handkerchiefs!"

Twenty-four hours later the traincar load of khaki-clad men poured out at the Dale station. A different crowd waited from those who had welcomed Luther. Now sturdy farmers and wives pushed to the front, eager to see husbands and sons. No bank clerk's false tribute but the spontaneous cheers from a hundred throats warmed the soldiers. Tears brighter than all the diamonds ever mined sparkled and brimmed in grateful eyes.

Tim swallowed a haystack-sized lump in his throat and eagerly searched the crowd for Hope. Friendly faces and slaps on the back melted much of his antagonism toward the town that had once condemned him. Had Sam Johnson been responsible, perhaps writing home of the medals for sharpshooting Tim had won? Yet as the crowd dispersed, Tim's heart sank. Luther Jones and Justin and Hope Farrell were conspicuous by their absence.

"Timothy, welcome home." A soft feminine voice that yet held authority turned Tim from his futile search of Main Street. Grace Forsythe held out a gloved hand. "If you'll come with me, please." She led the disappointed Tim straight to the charming cottage next to the library, opened the door, and motioned him to the cozy living room.

Tim quickly scanned the room. Empty, except for himself and his hostess. "Mrs.

Forsythe, why didn't Hope come to the station?" He removed his cap and stood turning it in his hands.

Blue eyes bright with indignation never wavered. Grace seated herself and indicated a chair for Tim. "Her father ordered her not to come," she said quietly.

Dull red streaks marred Tim's controlled face. His fingers tightened on the cap, twisting it out of shape.

"It's been very hard for Hope since the reception." Grace's soft white curls bobbed when she asked, "You know of that?"

"Yes." The word hung heavy and significant in the quiet room.

Grace stirred restlessly. "Justin Farrell thinks he can wear her down but he can't. First he tried shouting. He told Hope the day after the reception she might as well accept Luther for he had made a pact with Luther's father years before and promised Hope's hand."

Tim's mouth went dry. "What did she say?"

Satisfaction filled Grace Forsythe's features as she folded her hands calmly. "She told him he might have promised her hand but he could never promise her heart. She added that no human being — even a father — had the right to promise another's life in any way and that slavery ended with the Civil War."

Tim came alive in a hurry. He could almost envision Hope standing up to her father. *"And?"*

"She's been more or less confined to her room ever since. Justin allows her to come to the library and to see me." Grace's lip curled with scorn. "He knows well enough that I would have no qualms about telling the town he rules what he's up to if he goes too far." She fixed her steady gaze on Tim's face and he remembered how Sam Johnson related the librarian's understanding and kindness. The early loss of the husband she loved was etched in every delicate line on her lovely, tranquil face.

"What complicates things is Hope's tremendous faith in God and her belief in His commandments, especially to honor father and mother. She's having a hard time standing against Justin." She hesitated but her clear, direct eyes never left his face. "Tim, have you accepted the Lord?"

"No." All the bitterness of a lifetime rose in him.

"Why not? Don't you think you need Him where you're going?"

Tim felt himself squirm. "It seems a pretty shabby trick to ignore God for years

91

and then try and square things when the going gets rough," he mumbled.

She wouldn't let him off so easily. Her keen eyes softened and she placed a soft but strong hand on his. "Is that the real reason?"

He shook his head, wanting to tell her of the years when Hope's example and his mother's concern were quickly erased by Justin Farrell's Sunday-only religion and hypocrisy.

"It's all right, Tim. I don't blame you for feeling as you do."

He lifted blurred eyes and clutched her hand. The motherliness of her touched something in him that had died with Mary Wainwright and now struggled for new birth. He pressed his lips tight and wondered for the millionth time why the God Hope loved had let his mother die.

"Although Hope wants to be a dutiful daughter, her father has set limits far beyond what she can observe," Grace told him. "Be at the churchyard cemetery gates when it begins to grow dark. She will meet you there." Grace stood. "Do you need a place to stay?"

"No, ma'am." He got up and put on his cap. "The Johnsons expect me any time I get there." His pulse raced. "Thank you for being Hope's friend — and mine," he added softly.

"Tim." Her voice stopped him halfway to the front door. "Don't judge God by those who claim to know Him, only by those who do. And listen to what Hope says, will you?"

"I will." Tim felt he had just stepped from fog into bright sunlight and he impulsively pumped her hand and then walked out.

Past the bakery, the stable, and Miss Hattie's, past the butcher shop, mercantile, and grocery, even marching by the bank, Tim thrust his shoulders back and held his head high. *Let the whole town see him.* Not for Justin Farrell or any man would he skulk through back alleys. A faint enjoyment at the way Sam and Grampaw and the others would applaud if they could see him set a smile on his well-shaped lips.

Left, right, left, right. Suddenly his steps slowed, his smile froze. Just ahead Luther Jones stood holding open the gate to the Farrells' imposing yard and home. A slight figure in a gown the color of early spring sunlight dotted with tiny lavender flowers stepped through.

"Timothy!" Hope's glad cry made his heart race. With the utmost deference, he bared his head. "Hope." He held out his hand and she placed hers in it. Even through the lacy glove he felt her pulsing fingertips and the surreptitious squeeze.

"Hello, Wainwright." Luther Jones, ever his nemesis, slammed shut the gate and advanced toward him.

Thank God Luther wasn't in uniform. Tim had privately sworn never to salute his enemy. "Jones."

"What are you doing here? Did you desert — already?" The implication he would if he hadn't done so to date shook Tim. Now the self-discipline and army-imposed control, courtesy of Sergeant Kincaid, rose in triumph. "I'm the one in uniform, not you. It's good to see you, Hope." Tim saluted her, sent a look of love into her shining eyes, and marched away knowing he had scored a direct hit to Luther Jones's pride.

"Hope wanted to laugh," Tim confided to Sam after his long legs ate up the dusty road to the Johnson farm. "I could always tell. First her eyes shine then her face sort of crinkles up. I left while she could keep serious. No use making things tougher on her than they already are." His sense of elation vanished. "Must be hard being a girl."

"That's what my sisters say," Sam agreed, but his eyes crinkled up the exact way Hope's did when amused.

With a warning word to Sam not to mention his destination, Tim slipped away at dusk. He wanted to reach the rendezvous site before Hope could arrive. Once there, he straightened his cap, brushed his uniform, and wiped road dust from his shoes. Although darkness would hide untidiness, he must be as presentable as possible for Hope.

She came in a little rush, at least fifteen minutes after dark. Every moment had been a lifetime, wondering if she might not come at all. The sound of flying feet on the summer-parched grass that never stayed green in spite of buckets of carried water alerted him.

"Tim?"

"Here, my darling." In one stride his eyes, accustomed to the darkness, discovered her slender white form. He opened his arms and she ran straight into them. The starlight showed her white face, her eyes, her mouth. Tim gathered her close and kissed her. This time her response left no doubt. His arms tightened and wonder raced through him along with humility. How could one so pure, so precious, love Timothy Wainwright?

"I can't stay long," she whispered. "Father's suspicious and Luther follows me like a shadow. If there hadn't been a bank meeting I don't think I could have come. Father insisted that Luther attend." Her breath came in quick breaths.

"Hope, will you marry me?" All the carefully prepared speeches Tim had considered over the past days melted into the simple question.

"Someday, if-if —" Her voice broke into a sob.

"If what?" He gently tipped her chin up with one finger. "You said you loved me, the right way." His voice grew hoarse. "You — you haven't changed?"

"Never!" Some of her father's spirit arose in her and her arms tightened around him.

"Then what is it? Hope, I don't want to wait for someday. I want you to marry me now. While I'm home." He ignored her start of surprise. "Sam will help me arrange it. I'm twenty-one, a man. You're nineteen and old enough to choose." His hold on her slackened. He freed himself from her clinging arms and gently held her away from him, her hands clasped in his. "I-I wouldn't ask for a real marriage now." He could feel embarrassment lick at his veins but he went on doggedly. "That could wait until I get home. But, Hope —" He clutched her soft hands. "We're going overseas, probably soon. Will you let me go knowing you're my wife, at least in name? It would protect you from your father and Luther. I don't trust them. And do you think anything on earth could keep me from coming back when I know it's to you?"

The last thing he expected was tears, yet warm drops dripped down on their interwoven hands. "Oh Tim, I want to! I want to be your wife." She leaned against him. "But there's something between us that will shadow our lives."

"Not Luther! Your father?"

"They could never stop me." Pride rang through her words. "I'm a Christian. You aren't. To be unequally yoked can only bring pain and destroy us both." Her head drooped.

Tim had the feeling of being slowly iced. He had been willing to fight Justin, Luther, and the devil for Hope. But how could he fight God?

7

Tim dropped Hope's hands as if they were on fire. Waves of shock washed through him. He had expected hesitation and surprise, but nothing like this. "I always knew I could never be good enough for you," he said half under his breath.

"You know it isn't that!" Her low cry cut through his misery.

"Then don't let your religion stand between us," he pleaded and took her hands again. "You know I would never stop you from worshiping God in whatever way you chose. I'd never stand in your way, Hope. Why should it matter?" He managed a laugh that sounded unconvincing even to himself. "I don't suppose I'll get much chance to go to church in France or Germany but when I get back, I'll go every Sunday if you want me to." He felt her fingers tremble then she spoke rapidly. Her tone of voice told Tim she had thought about this a great deal.

"It isn't about going to church, Tim."

His spirits lightened but her next words plummeted him into the depths of despair.

"I belong to the Lord Jesus Christ. I gave myself to Him when I was eight years old. No matter how much I love you, He has to come first."

Tim's husky voice lowered even more. "Do you think I'd care? That I'm such a poor stick I'd be jealous or feel I only had your second best love?" He drew her close and peered down on her shadowed face. "Please, Hope, don't let your beliefs make a difference. Why, I believe in God too. Not the God Justin Farrell worships but the God I see in sunrises and sunsets and snowstorms and the forest. Isn't that enough?"

"It's a wonderful beginning," she said gently. Her upturned face shone in the pale starlight. "But nothing in heaven or earth can bring you salvation and eternal life except your own personal acceptance and knowledge of Jesus and that He came to save you."

Every word rang a death knell in Tim's heart. For a traitorous moment he considered pretending the belief Hope had outlined. Then he squared his shoulders. Even for her he would not abandon his scorn for deception and implied lies. "I wish I could

99

believe and accept —" To his amazement, he realized how true it was.

Hope's grasp on his arms tightened. "Then you will! Jesus says He will in no wise cast out those who come to Him."

Tim's heart soared again. "Then we can get married? If anyone can help me really find Jesus, it's you."

He felt rather than heard her little gasp and acted on it. "Sam Johnson is ready to help us. I'll be home for a week. If you'll just say yes, I'll arrange everything. That way, too, I'll have the right to send money home. We don't get paid a lot but I don't need much." Never had he pleaded his cause so well. "If things get too bad for you to stay at home, what I can send will allow you to be free."

She stirred in his arms but Tim placed one hand over her lips before she could speak. "Don't answer now. Just think about it. I know it's all new and strange, my darling, but remember, I'm just Tim who loves you." He kissed her, then with a feeling of renunciation held her at arm's length. "Come. I'll walk you home." He tucked her hand through the crook of his arm and started toward Justin Farrell's home, a home that should have been Tim's as well.

With one eye cocked for late passersby

who might report seeing them together to Hope's father, Tim led the now-silent girl home.

"Oh, no! Father's home!" Tim spurred the dismayed girl into action.

"Quick, around back." His keen eyes had already spotted lamplight streaming from the upstairs bedroom that belonged to Maura. He hurried Hope into the protective shade of the big fir tree outside his and Maura's windows then selected a few pebbles from the gravel path and took aim. Their familiar pitter-patter on the Irishwoman's window would bring help as it had done before when Tim didn't dare climb the tree for fear of getting pitch on his good clothes.

Maura's curtain opened a few inches and reclosed. Before long a flushed face beneath wild red hair appeared at the kitchen door. With one finger over her lips and a warning look in her blue eyes, Maura gave an impatient jerk of her hand.

"Goodnight, beloved," Tim whispered, and Hope smiled before vanishing inside the door.

"Maura, is that you? Get some coffee in here."

Huddled in the darkness Tim felt hot blood gush into his face at Luther's arrogant order. He bit his lip and lay low. Could

Hope escape to her own room without being discovered? His ears, turned to the slightest whisper, caught Maura's low, "Now, quietly," and heartbeats later a light appeared in Hope's room. Her slender form appeared at the open window and she leaned out, waved, and then closed the window and drew the drapes.

Tim found he'd been holding his breath. While he desperately wanted to march in and claim Hope, until she gave him a final answer he didn't have that right. He grinned in spite of himself. Nothing said he couldn't do a reconnaissance mission. The more he learned concerning Justin and Luther's plans, the better prepared he'd be. Tim crept back around the big house until he lay directly under the open library window, well hidden by the beautifully pruned rhododendrons. They had long since stopped blooming but the fresh green growth offered excellent cover. "More than I'll have at the front," Tim muttered grimly.

"Why didn't Hope wait up for us, Maura?" Luther must be standing right next to the window, Tim thought, and then the petulant voice demanded, "Where is she, anyway?"

"In her room." A rattle of china and silver followed.

"That will be all, Maura. You can clear up in the morning," Justin said.

"Thank ye." A swish of starched skirts told Tim Maura had gone. He remained in place while the unsuspecting men discussed bank affairs and the possibility of taking in someone to help while Luther was away. To his disappointment, neither mentioned Hope and at last Justin turned out the lights and Tim melted into the night, wondering what Hope's decision would be. . . .

Hope turned from the window, rushed into her night things, and got into bed. If no line of light crept from under her door she'd be saved a possible confrontation with Justin, Luther, or both. Her heart pounded and for a long time she simply lay still, savoring the knowledge Tim's love brought. The homage in his eyes when he looked down at her in the starlight left her shaken but joyous. Then remembrance of the gulf between them shattered her peace. What should she do? Would it be wrong to marry him under the circumstances? He asked so little — a wife in name only until he returned from the front. Could she bear to let him go away, perhaps never to return, without granting his request?

"I know he isn't far from You," she whispered to God in the still night. "I believe Your Holy Spirit will work with him until he accepts Your Son. What should I do?" A hundred scenes rose to confront her: Tim, marching valiantly into battle; herself, battered by her father's insistence that she marry Luther when she abhorred everything he stood for. Only last night he had waylaid her when she walked in the garden. His strong arms and seeking lips revolted her, as did the taint of whiskey on his breath.

"Let me go." She struggled to no avail.

"Never. I'm going to marry you."

"Why? You don't love me," she cried.

His usually half-closed eyes opened wide. Something flickered deep in their intense blue depths. "Strangely enough, I do. You'll like being an officer's wife. A lot better than being married to a doughboy like Wainwright." His lips curved in a smile and he kissed her in a way that left her slightly sick.

Hope wrenched free and ran, followed by his laughter. Could anything be worse than having to marry Luther Jones? He said he loved her but his kiss betrayed sheer lust, not the sacred feeling her own mother, then Mary Wainwright, had taught must be part of a Christian's marriage. She scrubbed her mouth hard with her handkerchief until it burned.

More scenes came to haunt her, past, present, even future, until she didn't know when awareness changed to troubled dreams. She awoke to bright sunshine feeling she hadn't slept at all. Dark shadows underscored her amber eyes and even Justin, who seldom noticed such things, remarked at breakfast, "Your early night doesn't seem to have helped."

Hope hid her fingers in her lap to keep from giving away her turmoil.

"By the way, Reverend Slater is coming over this afternoon." Justin rearranged his silver on the speckless white cloth. His mouth set in a grim line. "There will be no more of your tricks, Hope. Either you agree to setting a time very soon to marry Luther in church or we'll pack you off to a justice of the peace. I'm tired of your dithering and so is Luther."

Hope raised anguished eyes to her father. Every Scripture passage about honoring parents warred with those about what marriage must be. "I'm sorry, Father. I don't love Luther."

Justin actually looked shocked. "Be still! Decent girls don't talk about love before marriage. Once you belong to Luther, love will come."

"*Never.*" The denial sent unbelievable

strength into Hope. So did the memory of his using force in the garden. She would not, could not, endure a lifetime or even an hour of Luther's so-called love.

Justin shoved his chair back on the polished floor with such violence it overturned. His face settled into angry lines Hope knew only too well. "You will do as I say."

Hope searched her brain. She must have time, a reprieve. "Father, could Reverend Slater come in a few days instead of now?" she pleaded. "I've hardly had time to think since Luther arrived." She twisted her fingers until they turned white. "Besides, you know I'm involved in a lot of church and town activities. If I'm to be m-married I'll need to appoint others to fill in, and —"

Luther unwittingly came to her rescue. He set his empty coffee cup down and drawled, "I can wait. No wife of mine's going to be run ragged by Dale or any other town. She'll have enough to do just making me happy."

A primitive, un-Christian desire to slap his smug face left Hope shaken and only a silent, frantic prayer for strength kept her from dashing out the front door.

"*Well?*" Her father glared at her and Hope realized he'd spoken.

"I'm sorry, Father. What did you say?"

How much longer could she remain calm in the face of tyranny?

"I'll arrange for Reverend Slater to meet with us later," he said grudgingly and rose to his full, massive height. "Now that's settled, I want you to accompany me to the bank, Luther."

"Father?" Hope's small voice stopped his march to the door. "After I'm married, wh-where will I live?"

"Here, of course. This house is big enough for all of us and it's folly for Luther to be burdened with the expense of another home, especially when we don't know how long he will be gone. Come, son." He linked his arm in Luther's but not before the would-be bridegroom cocked one eyebrow leeringly at Hope.

Hope sat at the untidy breakfast table until Maura came in. "Ye won't be for obeyin', will ye?" She sank into a chair next to Hope, eyes anxious, her sturdy hand over the little white one.

"I can't." Even Hope's lips went white. "Marriage with Luther Jones would be hell."

"Then fly to your lad, child. He won't let such a thing happen." Maura's eyes deepened and moisture softened them.

The next hours and days blurred into a

time Hope would never be able to sort out completely. First a brief note was dispatched by a trusted neighbor boy who despised Justin Farrell and worshiped Hope. Hope didn't even sign the message that simply read,

I NEED YOU — RIGHT AWAY.

In the short time it took for the boy to bicycle to the Johnson farm and for Tim to reach the Farrell home, Hope fought a losing battle. She must marry Tim. She just didn't have the strength to vanquish her father and Luther. Surely Tim would learn to love his Lord! Once he did there would be time enough for themselves.

She met him in the shade of a great arch of roses, their heavy perfume filling the air with promise.

"I'm here, Hope." His quiet voice roused her from her thoughts. He made no effort to touch her but stood ramrod-straight, waiting for her to speak.

"Timothy." Her face became the shade of the palest roses. "You said if we married you wouldn't ask anything more for now." Painful red showed how hard it was for her to approach him. Yet she must.

"I meant every word of it." A new manliness had aged Tim but his steady dark eyes never wavered.

"Then I will marry you and pray to God for the day we can truly be one in spirit as well as in marriage."

With a glad cry, Tim bridged the grassy distance between them. An unearthly radiance transformed him and he bowed before her. "I will give my life before doing anything to hurt you," he pledged, his face as white as hers had been moments before. His kiss erased her fears and gladness sprang up within her.

"We must move swiftly," she explained when they sat down on a garden bench well hidden from the street. "I've convinced Father to wait a few days. Will that be enough time for us?"

Tim nodded. "Sam Johnson already checked. Dear, you can be Mrs. Timothy Wainwright before the end of the week. Then nothing your father or Luther can do will harm you." He almost added, *or the devil,* but caught himself in time. It didn't pay to defy Satan.

A potpourri of vivid memories mingled with the moment when Tim in his uniform and Hope in the white gown she once tore from her body stood before a minister in a small town near Dale. Maura had advised,

"Don't let the memory of that awful reception be for spoilin' the pleasure Tim will get from ye wearin' it."

She had also advised against going to Reverend Slater. "I'm not for saying he would give ye away but it doesn't pay to take chances." So instead of a wedding with all of Dale present, only Sam Johnson and Grace Forsythe stood with the couple. Maura confessed just before she smuggled the bride out, "It near breaks my heart not to be there but I'll stay here just in case. . . ."

The time-honored service seemed newly poignant. The kindly, sympathetic minister's voice asking, "Forsaking all others, keep thee only unto him, as long as you both shall live?" was followed by her low "I do," and Tim's ringing affirmative.

"I pronounce you man and wife. What God has joined together, let no man put asunder." The minister squeezed Hope's slim left hand with the shining gold band and turned to the tall soldier. "You may kiss your bride."

If Hope had doubted earlier, Tim's reverent kiss settled her as nothing else could have done. Mr. and Mrs. Timothy Wainwright, irrevocably joined together — for life.

"Well, Mrs. Wainwright?" Tim's bright

gaze fastened on his bride's dear face.

"It — it sounds nice." She turned the ring on her finger. "Hope Wainwright."

A little stir behind them and an unaccustomed look of gravity on Sam's face broke into their special moment. "I — uh — I hate to do this but I have to tell you something." He shuffled his feet, glanced down, then looked straight at Tim. "We're due back to Camp Lewis early. Word came to the farm this afternoon and I didn't want to say anything."

"Tomorrow?" Hope's voice cracked as she uttered the word.

"We leave on the morning train." He eyed them, then looked down. "You still have tonight." He turned away and stared at the plain wall of the pastor's study.

Hope knew she'd never forget the pain in Tim's face that must also be carved into her own. Their plan had been to spend their precious time in Grace's cottage. Grace had obligingly insisted she needed to visit a friend on the outskirts of Dale for a few days.

"Perhaps we should go see your father." Tim sighed. "You left a note, didn't you? When will he get it?"

"Not until after his club meeting this evening. Too late for him to scour the town and find me — us." Hope shivered and crept closer to her new protector. "All I said was that I'd be away overnight, staying at Grace's." A rush of color filled her face and she lowered her voice to a whisper. "You said Father — Luther — they mustn't know we're married in name only or Father might threaten an annulment."

Tim's face turned deadly serious. "No one must know."

"I promise." Inspiration struck her. "Tim, why go to Father now? You can leave in the morning on the train. I'll go home. But when Luther and Father try to marry me off —" A nervous giggle escaped. "I'll have our marriage certificate."

He scowled. "I'd be a coward to let you in for what's ahead alone."

"No." Hope shook her golden head until the short white veil she had hurriedly instructed Maura to make swayed. "It will be far worse if you are there." She clung to him. "Please, Tim?"

At last he gave in. They spent their wedding night sitting close to one another, sharing all their memories, good and bad. Her hand rested in his and her head fit against his shoulder. When dawn brightened the sky they knelt together and Hope prayed. "Dear Father, protect Timothy in every way while we're apart. Lead him to a full knowledge of Your Son that we may be Your children. Help us to live for You. In Jesus' name, Amen."

Tim's arm tightened around her shoulders. If she had asked him at that moment to accept her Lord, he wouldn't have hesitated. Yet deep inside gladness that she had not mingled with assurance that one day he would accept Christ for his own sake.

They said goodbye at Grace's, their love too precious to be observed by all of Dale. Hope kept her tears in her heart and sent Tim away with a smile. Once in the busy street he never looked back but she knew he carried with him the image of her still in her wedding gown that she had left on all during the night.

When the train whistle mourned in the distance, Hope let her tears come but not for long. She hastily bathed her eyes, donned a cotton dress brought to the cottage by Maura a few days earlier, and walked home. To her amazement Father and Luther still sat in the pleasant dining room. A smile of satisfaction lifted Justin's lips and Luther looked like a kid who'd found his Christmas gifts early.

"Good. You're here. Reverend Slater is on his way," Justin gloated.

113

So it had come. The moment Hope feared yet gloried in. If Timothy could face enemy guns and cannon fire, she could face her trials. Armed with the memory of Tim's steady march out the gate without once looking back, Hope raised her chin, looked at Luther, then Justin, and quietly said, "I am ready."

8

Wild thoughts raced through Hope's brain. Should she blurt out that she had married Tim before Reverend Slater arrived? No, she must make her startling announcement in the presence of a reliable witness. She caught Maura's reassuring nod when she brought in more coffee. It steadied her.

The doorknocker had never sounded more ominous to Hope and soon Maura ushered in a beaming Reverend Slater.

"Have a cup of coffee," Justin invited with an expansive gesture. "How about a second breakfast? I presume such a busy man as yourself must be ready for a break."

Hope stared at her father. She hadn't seen him display such geniality for as long as she could remember.

"Don't mind if I do." Reverend Slater sank into a chair and smiled at Hope. "The Johnsons called me early this morning. The Army canceled the rest of Sam's leave and they knew I hadn't had the opportunity to see him since he came home."

Hope felt herself congeal. Surely Sam wouldn't —

"Fresh bacon and eggs and toast, Reverend." Maura made a show of busyness and set a steaming platter in front of Reverend Slater whose mild eyes lit up with anticipation.

"That will be all, Maura. Close the door on the way out."

If looks could kill, Justin Farrell would be laid out and ready for burial, Hope thought when she saw Maura's angry face. The solid thud of the closing door emphasized her disgust.

Reverend Slater broke the awkward silence through a mouthful of bacon and eggs. "Any time you decide to dismiss Maura, there's room in our kitchen for her. Mrs. Slater's talents run more to organization than to cooking, I'm afraid."

Even Justin unbent enough to smile at the sally. Mrs. Slater's cooking skills had been a town joke for years but her happy personality and hard work on behalf of the church more than made up for it.

Reverend Slater practically licked his platter before wiping his mouth on the snowy napkin. "Now, let's get to the business at hand."

Please God, help me. I need You. . . .

The dining room door burst open. Grace Forsythe, in a pale blue morning gown, burst in waving a newspaper. "Justin Farrell, you are sly! To think you never once let on. Oh, don't frown at Maura. She couldn't keep me out."

"What are you talking about and what are you doing here? Can't you see I'm in conference?" Justin rose and drew his brows together menacingly.

Grace laughed easily and Hope clenched sweaty fingers under the immaculate tablecloth. Had Maura called in help? Had God sent Grace?

Blue sparkles danced in Grace's eyes. "You've stolen a march on the whole town. Just look at our morning paper." She spread it on the table and pointed to the blazing headline:

DAUGHTER OF ESTEEMED BANKER WEDS

"*What?*" Justin roared and snatched up the paper. He read aloud:

In a quiet and private ceremony last evening, Miss Hope Farrell, only daughter of Dale's leading citizen Justin Farrell, and Mr. Timothy Wainwright, stepson of Mr. Farrell, were joined in holy matrimony. Mr. Wainwright left on this morning's train to rejoin his unit at Camp Lewis.

Hope had never seen her father so routed. He wheeled toward her but again Grace intervened.

"It's too bad your honeymoon was cut short, Hope." Only her alert eyes conveyed prior knowledge. "I'd polished my cottage and stocked it for you. At least you had a few hours there together. But Justin, how like you not to breathe a word of this to anyone. The whole town's talking." Grace quickly turned to Luther. "Were you in on it, too? Everyone is betting the little joke you played at the reception was to bring these young people to their senses."

Grace rattled on, this time to Reverend Slater. "You'll have to forgive the way I tore in here when I'm sure you were to be told first. I felt proud to be in on the best-kept secret Dale has had in a long time."

How unlike Grace to chatter, Hope thought. Then her amber eyes widened. Of course! This would give Justin and Luther a way to save face, time to consider before they betrayed their total lack of knowledge concerning Hope's marriage.

"The milkman just hollered congratulations, Miss Hope," Maura volunteered from the doorway. "Excuse me, I mean Mrs. Wainwright." The telephone bell tinkled. "That's probably someone calling with good wishes. 'Twouldn't s'prise me if the whole town came callin' this morning."

Hope saw her father barely restrain a shudder before his quick mind grasped the situation and attempted to regain control. "Thank you for coming, Mrs. Forsythe. Reverend Slater, I'm sorry you weren't consulted." He shot a murderous look toward his daughter. "So little time, you understand." Still talking, he edged the visitors toward the doorway, leaving Hope to face Luther.

"Is it true?"

She shuddered at the ugly look on his face but forced herself to gaze straight at him and hold out the slender white hand that proudly wore Timothy's ring. "Yes."

"You'll pay for this." His lips curved into a snarl. "So will he. I swear by that God you pretend to worship. You — you —" Frustration and hatred choked off his voice. His hands grabbed her shoulders and his fingers dug in like the talons of an eagle. "You white-faced deceiver, in love with *him?*"

Superhuman strength flowed into Hope's

119

veins. With a mighty jerk she freed herself and stepped so the dining room table stood between them. "Yes. Since he first came to us. First as his sister, now as his wife." She hurled the words like bullets and gloated when she saw they found their mark.

The closing of a door broke the intense moment. Haggard and menacing, Justin strode back into the room. "You *dared* mock me. You *dared* marry against my wishes. Then you *dared* put that announcement in the paper for everyone to see —"

"I didn't put it in the paper." Hope couldn't help being sorry for him in spite of her fear.

"Then who did? That meddling Forsythe woman? Your precious husband?" He clenched and unclenched his hands at his sides.

"Who cares?" Luther bellowed. "What matters is what you're going to do now. Get the marriage annulled. I tell you, she's mine. You promised my father."

"It's too late." Justin steadied himself against a chair back. Great drops of sweat beaded his forehead. "A half-dozen people have already expressed their delight. I never thought Dale had any use for Timothy but the war has made a difference." He mopped his face with a white handkerchief. "Besides, they stayed at the Forsythe place last night." Anger flared. "Hope, why did you do this to me?"

Her compassion died. Righteous indignation replaced it. "What were you doing to me, forcing me to marry a man I could never respect? Father, I *love* Timothy and he loves me, the way you must have loved my mother."

For a single heartbeat softness crept into his eyes. It warred with pride — and lost. "We'll discuss this later. Luther, come with me. If ever we needed to hold our heads high, it's now. I will not have this town I rule laughing behind my back, or yours."

"But what about me?" Luther protested bitterly, his voice a childish whine.

"You will do as I say." Justin drew himself up and glared at his spurned favorite. A tiny muscle in his jaw quivered. To Hope's amazement, Luther sullenly followed the older man out without a word.

"Well, the spalpeen's had his nose rubbed in the dust," Maura rejoiced as soon as the men slammed out the front door and she could get back to her charge.

Like a match to shavings, her comment touched off a wellspring inside Hope. She buried her face in her hands until the laughter ended in cleansing, healing tears and Maura patted the golden head. "I'm thinkin' how your lad would be proud," she whispered. "Why don't ye trot along and write to him so he'll be sure of gettin' it before he gets sent out?"

Hope's mirth and tears subsided. "I will, but Maura, did you call Grace? And how did the paper learn about us?"

Maura's ruddy cheeks turned even redder. "Seemed to me ye'd be needin' some support," she admitted. "I called for Mrs. Forsythe but I didn't be for puttin' the notice in the paper."

Later that afternoon Hope slipped down Main Street and into the library. No patrons haunted it at closing. "Grace, dear, did you put the announcement in the paper? Or — did Tim?"

The curly white head shook decidedly. "No, but I know who did."

"Really?" Hope scooted to the edge of her chair. "Who?"

"Sam. He remarked after the wedding that he had dropped off a little note at the newspaper office. It didn't completely register at the time, what with the news the boys had to go back this morning. The moment the paper came I realized what he meant and was ready to come to your place when Maura called."

Hope swallowed a lump in her throat and blinked hard. "I hated to deceive Father, learning that way and everything."

Grace's no-nonsense voice perked her up. "It's better this way. He had warning so he could meet the surprise, perhaps even let on without actually saying so that he knew it all along."

"You provided him with that opportunity," Hope reminded gratefully and smoothed a crease in her skirt.

"No one should be deliberately humiliated unless there is no other way to handle things," Grace said quietly. "How he chooses to act from now on will largely determine his continuing prestige in Dale. He's wise enough to know it too." She finished shelving the last of the returned books, waited for Hope to go out, and then locked the library door behind her. "Now, run along and don't start having regrets. The love of a good man is one of God's most precious gifts."

She paused with her hand still on the library doorknob and looked past Main Street, past the low hills surrounding the town to the snow-capped peaks in the distance. Hope had the feeling her friend saw much farther, back to a time when a young man offered his love and was accepted. "It's worth whatever price you have to pay to know what marriage as God ordained, a true becoming one, is. Child, don't look back."

For the second time, Hope saw Timothy marching away without regrets, buoyed by the knowledge she loved and prayed for him. Her heart gave a great lurch. He must come back. In the meantime, she must face her father without apology or excuse.

The interview after supper proved worse than anything Hope had anticipated. Perhaps if Luther had left father and daughter to talk things out it could have been armed truce rather than outright war. But Luther had eluded Justin's watchful eye in late afternoon and succeeded in finding enough liquor to float a battleship. By the time he came down late for dinner, in defiance of every rule Justin lived by, he positively reeked of whiskey.

"You're drunk!" Justin roared. "Things are bad enough without you taking to the bottle. I won't have it in my house, do you understand?"

"I'm a grown man and I'll do as I please." The whiskey evidently gave Luther both belligerence and courage. "Everyone drinks a little now and —"

"No one drinks in this house. Get upstairs

and stay there until you can act like a gentleman."

"A gentleman. He wants a gentleman. Well, you've got one, Justin Farrell, a real gentleman son-in-law."

"Don't speak to me like that," Justin thundered. "And get upstairs."

Luther gathered his remnants of outraged dignity and staggered toward the door. "It's all her fault," he spat and glared at Hope. "Leading a man on to distraction, playing with him, what do you expect?" He slammed out.

"See what you've done." Any wish for a quiet talk vanished.

Hope took a long, quivering breath and steadied her voice. "I? Father, if you only knew Luther as I do, you'd never say such a thing."

"So you're harping on lies you've heard and believed about my son," Justin accused, his eyes hard. "He's right. If you had married him the night of the reception as we planned, do you think he'd be in this abominable condition? He's heartbroken and you have the audacity to sit in judgment on him."

"He isn't heartbroken. Luther's never loved anyone except himself. He's just angry because I'm something that belongs to Timothy that Luther can't take away, as he took toys and reputation long ago."

For a moment she thought he would strike her. Instead he rose and towered over her, casting a dark shadow in the lamplit room that made her feel defenseless. Then he said, "I have decided what to do with you, but you have a choice. You can either agree to an annulment and swear you have grounds for it, then marry Luther, or you can get out. I'll have no daughter who defies me."

A blush rose from the modest neckline of Hope's simple muslin gown and spread throughout her face. A tiny pulsebeat wavered in her temples.

"Well?" Like an instrument of retribution Justin loomed above her.

"I cannot do that."

"As of this moment I have no daughter. Pack and go. I don't care where."

Strange that in the middle of her pain, concern for his terrible pride rose in Hope. "What will you tell people?"

He snapped to rigid attention. "No one dares question what I do." His face darkened until he resembled an eagle Hope once saw, flying above his domain, but flying alone.

Justin rang the silver bell that summoned Maura. She responded with such alacrity Hope knew she must have been lingering near the door. With autocratic formality Justin pronounced sentence. "Hope is to leave this house tonight. Pack her clothing and see that it is delivered to wherever she chooses to go. You may either go with her or stay. But if you do, you are never again to mention her name in my presence."

"Oh, sir, ye'd not be for sendin' her away!" The habit of silence couldn't withstand Maura's fear and anger.

"Be quiet, woman! Now get out, both of you." The very fact he made no effort to lower his voice in spite of the open windows showed Justin Farrell's strain.

Maura stood aside and let Hope precede her into the hall then up the interminable stairs to the sanctuary of the girl's room. Hope didn't shed one tear. She simply snatched clothes from her closet and out of drawers, feverishly folding them into neat piles. Dumbfounded by the rapid turn of events, Maura procured a large valise and some bags that would hold what Hope needed until a drayman delivered the trunk. She disappeared once and returned with news for Hope.

"Mrs. Forsythe is expectin' ye."

Hope's lips trembled but she set them in an uncompromising line. Feelings could come later. Now she must flee before Luther learned what happened and came to her door.

When Maura left Hope at the cottage door she humbly asked, "What would ye be for havin' me do? Stay? Or go?"

The exhausted girl tried to focus on Maura's plight instead of her own. "I don't know."

"Reverend Slater did mean it," Maura reminded. "They'd be glad to have me do for them." Not a change in tone hinted at a preference.

Hope threw herself into Maura's freckled, rounded arms. "Would you stay, Maura? He's still my father."

The housekeeper hugged her. "I'll stay — for ye. Sure, and he can't help but be regrettin' his hastiness. It's his awful proudness that's to blame. Someday he'll be forced to admit what a spalpeen he's admired." She sighed." 'Til then, ye can only pray and I'll be for takin' care of him. Luther will go soon. When he does, himself will have time to think."

Hope watched the faithful figure disappear into the growing dusk, cheered by Maura's words. Her father could cast her off, consider he no longer had a daughter, even refuse to speak if they met on the street. But he could never keep his daughter from loving — and praying — for him.

9

The second time Timothy Wainwright, Sam Johnson, Grampaw, and the others swung onto the train for Camp Lewis, the good-natured jeers and boasting were now in the past. The first few clacking miles sped by in silence. Then Sam Johnson pulled an early morning edition of the local paper from his pocket, eyed Tim with a warning glance, and said, "Hey, boys, wanta hear something interesting?"

"What could be more interesting than getting back to our loving Sergeant Kincaid?" Grampaw asked sourly.

"This." Sam triumphantly read out loud, *"Daughter of Esteemed Banker Weds!"*

Tim froze. What on earth —

"Aw, Miss Hope didn't go and marry that poor fish Luther Jones, did she?" someone wailed. "Why'd she do that?"

"Huh, if she did, you can bet her pa planned it," Grampaw snorted. "He thinks God created Luther Jones special to be his son-in-law and succeed him in the bank. Well, the day he does, I'll bury my money in a hole rather than let Jones get his hands on any of it, Justin Farrell or no Justin Farrell."

"Wait," Sam protested. "She didn't marry Luther."

"Good for her! Who had spunk enough to get her out away from her daddy?" Grampaw demanded, eyes bright with glee.

Sam's eyes danced and Tim held his breath waiting for the tornado to hit.

"According to the paper," Sam drawled, " '*In a quiet and private ceremony last evening, Miss Hope Farrell, only daughter of Dale's leading citizen Justin Farrell, and Mr. Timothy Wainwright. . . .*' "

A shout drowned out the rest of the announcement. "Tim? *You* married Hope Farrell? *Hurrah for Tim!*" The car rang with congratulations, questions, and cheers.

"How come you didn't invite us?"

Tim couldn't answer but Sam did. "Come on, buddies, think even Tim could carry it off with a bunch of roughnecks like you cluttering up the countryside? Besides, he had me for best man so he didn't need any of you." A general shout of derision let Tim off the hook. When the roar subsided he whispered to Sam, "Did you put it in the paper?"

Sam tried to look innocent and failed miserably. "Well — I got to thinking even Justin Farrell shouldn't have to face what Dale could dish out if they knew he wasn't in on it." He crossed his eyes and wrinkled his nose. "Guess all that stuff Reverend Slater preaches about loving our enemies must have rubbed off a little bit."

Tim grunted and promptly forgot everything except Hope. He'd heard folks say every bride was beautiful but his heart denied that any girl or woman ever presented such a vision of sheer loveliness as his wife. Even the title had the power to fill the empty spot left years ago when Tim's mother died. *His wife. Hope Wainwright.* He leaned his head against the worn train seat, closed his eyes, and dreamed. They belonged to one another. Should he not come home, his last conscious moment would be one of fierce rejoicing.

"All's off that's gettin' off." The conductor's bellow rudely shook Tim out of his reverie. He automatically reached for his bag and followed Sam and the others back into the real world. How he wished he could see Luther Jones when he read that blazing headline and realized that, for once, he had lost to his enemy.

"Reckon if I'd up and snatched off the purtiest gal in Dale, I'd grin like a monkey, too," Grampaw cajoled. Amid the laughter that followed, Tim swung down from the train and headed for the barracks with his comrades from Dale.

Luther Jones never made idle threats. Even before he got drunk and disgraced himself before Hope and Justin a plan of revenge had taken root in his fertile brain and begun to grow. He awakened from his stupor amazingly clearheaded and remorseful — not for getting drunk, but for alienating Justin. He presented himself at the breakfast table debonair and as pleasant as could be expected of him.

"I want to apologize to you for my condition last night." Justin's brows shot skyward.

Putting all the pathos he could into his voice, Luther continued. "A man does things when he's hurt that he wouldn't do at other times. Can you forgive me?"

A look of relief softened Justin's harsh features. "It's understandable," he agreed gruffly. "But I'll have no more of it in my home. Not even by you, son."

"Where's Hope?" Luther veiled his anxiety.

"She is no longer my daughter." Every trace of relenting fled from Justin and he went rigid. "I ordered her to swear she had grounds for an annulment or leave. Maura packed her things and delivered her somewhere — probably to that meddling Forsythe woman's home — after you went upstairs last night."

Luther's long-suppressed sense of decency struggled to assert itself. "But why?" he demanded, pity for Hope overruling his own desires. "Don't you know that will make her even more stubborn? If you had let her stay, in time she would have given in. She couldn't have held out against both of us."

Justin hesitated and pursed his lips, then shook his head. "Until yesterday I'd have agreed with you. Not now." He abruptly rose and threw down his napkin, ignoring the fact his well-prepared breakfast remained largely uneaten. "We both have to forget her." His face twisted but his eyes stayed flinty.

Luther cleared his throat. "I've been thinking. . . ."

"Yes?"

"Perhaps we shouldn't blame her too much. Remember, she and Timothy grew up together. If he insisted on their getting married . . ." His shrug eloquently completed the sentence.

"That —" Justin, who never swore, uttered a rough oath.

Luther's jaded heart leaped. He eagerly leaned forward. "How much influence do you have with those in high places?"

Justin immediately reverted to his usual haughty state. "You know the answer to that." He opened then closed his big hand into a gesture of control. "Why?"

His protégé calmly ate a bite of delicious pancake then said, "I know how to make Timothy Wainwright wish he had never heard of Justin Farrell and his family."

"Well?" Twin flames lit Justin's fanatical eyes.

"This is what I have in mind, but you'll have to work hard and it has to be fast, within the next day or two." He outlined the diabolical plan that had come into full bloom with such far-reaching ramifications Justin forgot himself enough to drop back into a chair and refrain from interrupting although a dozen questions hung on his lips.

"Can we — can you do it?" Luther demanded, his blue eyes glowing.

A mighty hand shot out. "I can and will." Pact sealed, the two men hurried away from the house and down Main Street. As Luther predicted, they had much to do and little time in which to accomplish it.

Hope caught a glimpse of them from Grace Forsythe's yard. Gowned in a blue and white wash dress, she had gone out to pick a few posies for the breakfast table. Sunlight slanted off her gold ring and reminded her the hazy events of the past two days were no mirage. Neither were the stocky figures walking Main Street as if they owned it, as indeed, Justin Farrell did.

Unexpected pain replaced the anger and sympathy for her father that had kept her going while she told Grace what happened. Too tired to worry more, she'd fallen asleep in the simply furnished little white room Grace offered. The trill of a robin awakened her early. For a moment, she didn't know where she was or why, and then everything rushed back.

If her father saw her would he pass by with a glacial look? Hope couldn't bear to chance it so she hastily gathered the bright, dew-covered flowers and hurried inside.

Grace left for the library shortly after breakfast. "Now, I know you won't be happy if you're idle. I have an idea about that, but until I can get it arranged, would you like to be my housekeeper? You can start by doing the breakfast dishes, then choose what you want from the pantry and icebox and plan our dinner. I come home between one and two."

Soft arms encircled the kindly, older

woman. Amber eyes looked deep into determined blue ones and Hope said, "I love you so much!"

"I love you, too, child. Now let me run along or my record of opening on time will be spoiled." Grace hugged Hope and disappeared out the front door but not before calling back, "If you need anything just run over to the library!"

Hope enjoyed washing the pretty breakfast dishes, shaking off crumbs for the variety of birds that inhabited the backyard, and rinsing the dish towels and hanging them out to dry in the sun. She made her bed and swept and tidied the rest of the cottage. She smiled when she peeked through the open door at Grace's bedroom. Not so much as a piece of lint marred the perfect order.

On to raid the larder, Hope's spirits couldn't remain low on such a glorious day! God stayed in charge of the world even when poor creatures like herself had a hard time seeing His hand in what befell them.

A light tap at the door brought a wave of dread to Hope. Surely Luther wouldn't come here! She dried her hands on her apron and sped to the door.

"Here's your trunk, Miss Hope. Beg your pardon, Mrs. Wainwright." The drayman's friendly grin settled Hope's fears. He shifted the trunk's position on his brawny shoulders. "Where do you want it?"

"Right in here." She led the way. He heaved it off and into the corner of her room.

"Mighty pretty room. It's awful nice of you to come stay a spell with Miz Forsythe." He scratched his whitened head. "Never thought about it, but I guess she does get lonesome."

Hope almost blurted out that she didn't know what he meant but a familiar voice from the little hall spun her around.

"We'll be for missin' her at the big house but what with Timothy gone and Luther leavin' soon, it's nice for her to have a change." Warning signals flashed from Maura's Irish blue eyes and she smiled at the drayman. "Thanks for bein' so prompt."

His face turned red and Hope remembered how once long ago this man told around how Maura Cullen was a "fine figger of a woman" and if he dared, he'd go courtin' her. Maura had made short work of such ideas then and now she briskly shooed him out with a quick, "We won't keep you from your work. Thanks again." He backed out after stuttering, "Any time you need help, I'll be around."

"He will, too," Maura confirmed the moment the front door closed behind him. "Now, how are ye holding up?" Her approving glance swept the room. "Smaller than at home but a lot happier. Himself's tellin' those who ask that Grace Forsythe invited ye for 'an extended visit' since your new husband got called back." Grudging admiration lightened her grim expression. "It's the truth, of course, just not all of it."

Maura stayed until just before having to fly back and make sure lunch was on the table.

"Y-you won't get in trouble for coming, will you?" Hope asked.

Maura's Irish temper flared. "No man, includin' himself, tells me where I go when my work's done!" She lovingly patted Hope's hair. "An' if I choose to do that work faster, then what's it to anyone?" She sighed and started for the door. A troubled look replaced her defiance. "Hope, I fear Luther and himself are plotting something." Intense concentration wrinkled her still-smooth forehead. "I can't say what for I'm not knowin' — yet. But when the two of them get their heads together the way they did at breakfast, breakin' off when I came in, watch out."

"What else can they do?" Hope asked and

shrugged her shoulders. "Father has dis-
owned me, although he evidently isn't
telling the town. There isn't much left, is
there? They can't hurt Timothy. To get at
him means taking on the whole U.S.
Army." A watery smile lifted some of
Maura's gloom. "I doubt that even Father
or Luther can do that!"

"Don't be too sure," Maura advised, her
eyes keen and piercing. Then, as if she regretted mentioning it, she hastily added,
"Don't fret. Menfolk's bound to be per-
snickety when they're crossed."

Unsure whether to be cheered or more
depressed, Hope concentrated on lunch.
Small new potatoes and peas from the
garden, creamed the way Maura taught her.
A plate of delicately sliced ripe red toma-
toes. Tiny beaten biscuits served with fresh
homemade butter and strawberries also
from the garden.

"What a lovely sight!" Grace stood in the
small dining room doorway and surveyed the
spotless cloth, shining china, and silver. "I
usually don't go to all this bother for lunch."

Hope's face flushed with pleasure and
from the heat of the oven. "You have five
minutes to wash up, mum." She smiled.
"Your new cook won't have her biscuits
burn or sog from waiting."

"Fine thing," Grace grumbled and turned away with a twinkle in her eye. "The help you get today just doesn't know its place. Or if it does, it won't stay in it." She sighed exaggeratedly. "I can see now who will rule the home you and Timothy make when he comes back!"

Her parting shot turned Hope even rosier and set her heart to pounding. Her home and Timothy's, what a wonderful sound. A whiff from the kitchen instantly vanquished her dreams and she slid the pan of biscuits out just before they got too brown and arranged them on a pretty plate.

"Hope, how would you like to work in the library?" Grace inquired after dinner. Her direct blue gaze brought surprise to the younger woman's face.

"Why, I don't know. Could I?"

"Why not? I control it," Grace retorted. "Besides, since according to the town criers of Dale you've come to visit me for 'an extended visit,' isn't it natural I'd want to see more of you than is possible between library duties?"

"So you've heard." Hope bowed her head.

"Oh, yes." Grace laughed. "I've also had at least six inquiries about my health and if your 'visit' is really because I've been ailing."

"Aunt Grace, that's dreadful!" Hope gasped. "Oh dear, I'd forgotten the Dale gossips."

"I think it's amusing," Grace reassured her and stretched. Her warm smile erased Hope's feeling she might be annoyed. "So do I get myself an assistant librarian? You know, Hope, someday — hopefully a long time in the future — I'll want to retire. I'd like to leave the library to you, along with my savings. They'd be enough to keep you going in case —"

In case Timothy doesn't come home," Hope said quietly. She bit her lip but her hands remained steady. "I know it can happen, even though he promised to come home."

"Why don't we talk about it another time?" Grace suggested. She stood and settled her thin dark blue skirt. "I must get back to the library. If you haven't already done so, this afternoon's a good time to write a letter."

Hope hurried through lunch dishes, put a beef roast on the back of the stove to slow cook, and pared vegetables. She whipped up a rice custard in record time and soon settled down at the little desk in the pretty living room and began to write. Little tendrils of gold hair escaped their pins and made a halo around the sweet face, intent on her task.

141

Timothy received her letter after the worst training session they'd endured. Ever since being called back early, Sergeant Kincaid relentlessly drilled them. His stern demands for their best told the men of Dale how soon he expected company D to be shipped to the front. Something wild in Timothy exulted; a dirty job lay ahead. It had to be done or the world America and other peaceful countries knew would vanish forever. All he wanted to do was go complete the job and come home. Yet at times stories of those who had gone, fought, and returned haunted him. Bayonets and cannon fire. Bombs and dogfights in the air. Mud and filth and little if any sleep. Periods when all a man could do was keep on fighting until relieved, although the reason why a certain stretch of land was so important faded into the reality of war. Mustard gas, shell shock, and death were on the horizon.

As usual, Timothy retreated to read his letter. A September downpour had sidelined the soldiers to the barracks where they lay grumbling about everything from the food to the weather and a multitude of things in between. Tim slipped inside the base chapel with his letter. He'd been able to attend a few times but Hope's face interfered with his worship, if it could be called that. The chaplain was a good enough fellow but he couldn't compete with memories.

Now he slipped into a rear seat and let the peace of the building still him before slitting the envelope. Many pages floated out and he read slowly, living with Hope the events she had experienced on the day he boarded the train back to camp.

He wanted to cheer when Grace took control, ably assisted by Maura. He muttered under his breath, mindful of his surroundings, at Luther's drunken accusations. Fury rose within him when Justin offered his ultimatum; pride threatened to overwhelm him at Hope's refusal to comply with her father's commands. Someday there would be a reckoning, a final judgment where Justin must answer for his deeds. The satisfaction it brought to Tim was almost enough to make him believe!

Later Tim folded the thick letter and placed it in his shirt over his heart, next to the treasured testament Hope had given him. He stepped from the chapel and into the rain, little heeding it. With Hope's love and faith in him, he could face anything — the Huns, privation, even Kaiser Bill himself.

The strange idleness of the men halted him just inside the door of the barracks. No card games. No low chatter or loud talk. Just the men of Dale lying or sitting on their bunks.

"Did somebody die? Kaiser Bill, I hope." Tim's flippancy was lost in the silence.

"That'd be good news," Grampaw grunted.

Why should an unexplained dread grip Tim's throat? He turned searching eyes toward Sam Johnson, who, as usual, held center stage. "Well?"

Not a trace of Sam's boyish good humor escaped his tight lips. "Our Commanding Officer got transferred."

Tim relaxed. "So we still have Sergeant Kincaid, don't we?"

No one laughed and Tim's muscles tightened up. "Who's our new CO?" He held his breath. A wild thought crossed his mind. No, fate could never be so cruel. Did his face mirror his suspicion?

Sam's voice had never sounded so ominous. "You guessed it. Luther Jones."

10

Autumn 1917, America at war. A time of waving flags, a time of hope, pride, and despair. A time of prayers that good would soon triumph over evil. In American living rooms from coast to coast Victrolas blared such popular songs as "It's a Long Way to Tipperary," "Pack Up Your Troubles in Your Old Kit Bag," and "Keep the Home Fires Burning," their lyrics echoing the undercurrents of war. The great George M. Cohan's inspiring tune, "Over There," rose to the heights of popularity and remained a talisman in American homes.

Alice-blue gowns, so named for Alice Roosevelt Longworth, Teddy's daughter and the Capitol's darling, were the rage. Teddy Roosevelt put aside his dislike of President Wilson for not entering the war sooner against Germany and sought permission to raise a division of troops to fight in France, but to no avail.

Peace-loving President Wilson abhorred

war and had desperately tried to avoid being drawn in. Yet, once the die had been cast, he proved himself as great a leader in wartime as in peace. He touched hearts everywhere with his powerful declarations on behalf of the Allied cause and never failed to speak of the need to make a better world once the hellish battles ended.

Silent film stars aided the war cause. If courageous Lillian Gish or Norma Talmadge could wear the Red Cross worker's khaki uniform and serve in a hut in France, how much more could theatregoers, who lived what they saw, do for the war effort? Mary Pickford, Douglas Fairbanks, Sr., Charlie Chaplin, and many others spoke at rallies and delighted the crowds who bought Liberty Bonds.

Schoolchildren joined the Junior Red Cross. Young women served as nurses' aides. The cover of the June 1917 issue of *Ladies' Home Journal* featured a painting of a Red Cross nurse and an appealing war dog and touched off a fervor of patriotism that swelled the ranks of volunteers.

Autumn 1917, Hope Wainwright at war. Her private battles — with herself, the world, and, silently, with her father — seemed to abate as she settled into her library work. Books had long been among her best friends. Now she delighted in sharing those friends with the townspeople who needed something to lift their burdens.

"You'll love the *Five Little Peppers* series," she told her youthful patrons. "And see here? *Mary Ware in Texas*, another of the *Little Colonel* series. After you finish those, you'll be ready for the *Texas Bluebonnet* books, then those by Louisa May Alcott." She pointed to the well-worn copies of *Little Men* and *Little Women*. Male readers most often asked for Jack London's *Call of the Wild* or Zane Grey's *Riders of the Purple Sage*. Boys grabbed the Horatio Alger "from rags to riches" stories. Grace Livingston Hill's Christian romance novels went out as fast as they came back, with a waiting list for every title. Her inspiring stories based on high ideals glorified God and gained wide popularity.

Hope giggled to Grace one day at lunch. "You really get to know people by what they read. I wouldn't have believed that Mr. Wilson, the milkman, dotes on the classics while Miss Hattie can't wait to get her hands on anything with Sherlock Holmes in it!"

"Or that the butcher only reads plays, preferably pretwentieth-century ones, and Sam Johnson's parents take out as many books as they can carry, regardless of type." Her blue eyes twinkled. "The stories I could tell you! But you'll have more fun getting to know your fellow Dale-ites without my gossip." Her laughter died. "Hope, you're in an almost impossible situation. Are you feeling any happier?"

The wistfulness in her friend's voice halted any complaint the girl might have. "I'm happy sometimes, when I forget the terrible Third Battle at Ypres that's still raging. The British and French have pounded the Germans yet so far they haven't won." Ready tears appeared and she swallowed hard. "What's so terrible is the destruction of the drainage system from Allied bombardment before the infantry attack and then the heavy rains. Thousands of British soldiers drowned in the resulting swamp."

"I know." Grace laid her hand over Hope's. "We just have to keep praying and hanging on, dear."

Hope blinked. "It's just that those soldiers could be ours. Timothy, Sam, even Luther. . . ." She stared unseeingly out the window where red and gold leaves lazily floated in the fall air. "It's hard to believe here in this peaceful, beautiful place that somewhere in the world men are bleeding and dying."

A long sympathetic silence ended when Hope visibly pulled herself together. "The other thing is Father. He doesn't look at all well. Maura says he picks at his food; she thinks he's grieving. I wonder if I should try to see him."

"You will have to do what you feel is right," Grace advised. She rose and gathered soiled dishes from the table. Hope quickly collected the remaining food and carried it to the kitchen. Why hadn't she heard from Timothy? There had been nothing in the paper about company D being shipped out. She sighed. Men went to war; women waited. Sometimes she ached to be a man, free to volunteer. She'd never be a slacker. Any able-bodied man who refused to fight for his country deserved all the scorn he received.

A sudden thought halted her on her way to the pantry. Was she a slacker for not trying to straighten out things with her father?

That settled it. This evening when Father would be sure to be home she would go to see him.

A few hours later, gowned in the pale yellow gown she had admired what seemed centuries ago in Miss Hattie's shop window, Hope walked the short distance between Grace's cottage and the imposing Farrell house. Strange how it seemed a world away. She had been a child, then a schoolgirl there. Now a woman retraced the familiar steps knowing she could never go back.

"Why — Hope, child!" Maura met her at the door. She gulped, cast a fearful glance at the open study door off the hall behind her, then tugged Hope inside. She marched determinedly down the hall and into the dimly lit room. "Miss Hope's here, sir."

Hope barely had time to note the change in her father before his familiar voice chilled her. "I know no Miss Hope. Tell the person who has come I am not at home to her — now or ever."

Hope couldn't bear it. Since she left she had avoided being near enough her father to offer him the choice of speaking or ignoring her. Even at church she slipped in just before the final bell and back out during the closing prayer. Although she knew tongues had begun wagging about the length of her extended visit to Grace, the need to protect Justin Farrell from exposure ran strong in her veins.

Now she didn't hesitate. "Father, please, don't say that. I am still your daughter." She ran across the beautiful floor and threw herself on her knees before him, daring to rest her hot forehead on his knee. "Luther is gone. Timothy is gone." She felt the involuntary stiffening of his body and realized she had made a grave mistake in her choice of appeal. "Father, we only have each other. Can't we be friends?"

The world held its breath and waited for Justin's reply. Hope sensed a little shiver of torment and indecision rack her father. She awaited his verdict, silently praying as she had never prayed before.

His words fell like icicles from lips that had whitened even as she spoke. "I have no daughter."

Hope slowly shrank from him. The habit of years past when she refrained from speaking her mind to avoid conflict still held. Without another word, she rose, looked deep into Justin's expressionless eyes, then squared her shoulders and walked out of the room and the house, not even bidding Maura goodbye.

Left, right. Left, right. Was this how a defeated soldier felt? Pain filled her and her cadence faltered. Someone called an invitation from a porch filled with people. Hope responded but shook her head. She must not break down here. If she were forced to talk, to join in a discussion of the war, the pride holding her together might unstick. If no meeting occupied the church, she would go there.

But even that solace was denied. Brilliant light streamed from the open door and the sound of untrained but well-blended voices singing, "Saviour, Like a Shepherd Lead Us," made Hope pause. In the shadows of a tall hemlock between the church and the cemetery gates where she had secretly met Tim, her voice struggled to join in.

"We are thine, do thou befriend us;
Be the guardian of our way;
Keep thy flock, from sin defend us;
Seek us when we go astray."

Every word pierced her heart like an arrow. Sin and pride had entered her father's soul to make him cast her off. She thought of his face, thin and gaunt. Why must life be so hard?

The final words of the beloved old hymn* that had comforted worshipers for so many years now bestowed peace on Hope.

"Blessed Jesus, blessed Jesus,
Thou hast loved us, love us still;
Blessed Jesus, blessed Jesus,
Thou hast loved us, love us still."

* "Saviour, Like a Shepherd Lead Us" has been attributed to Dorothy Thrupp.

152

Hope was suddenly reminded of a memory verse she had learned long ago: *"I will not leave you comfortless: I will come to you."**

She had God's promises and the love of her Lord Jesus. The Guardian of her way had not and would not fail her in this time of need.

Autumn 1917, Timothy Wainwright at war. Sam Johnson's grim announcement that Luther Jones had been assigned company D's Commanding Officer settled over the men of Dale like a shroud. More and more Tim learned, even through his own intense bitterness, how little Luther was liked — either here or in his hometown. If Luther knew it, it could account for his new arrogance, far beyond anything even Timothy had seen from him.

"How do you stand it?" Sam burst out late one evening when they chanced to be alone for a few minutes. "Since that skunk arrived you've been given every dirty job there is. Why don't you tell him to go to the devil?"

"Our CO?" Tim's ugly laugh shattered the hazy autumn evening. "That's just what he's waiting for. How far do you think I'd get?

* John 16: 18(KJV)

Wouldn't Luther Jones just love to see me drummed out of the service, dishonorably discharged? It would give him a chance to brag how he either made men out of his troops or they turned yellow and quit."

"Yeah." But Sam's quick mind seized on something. "I bet Sergeant Kincaid'll do what he can. Why don't you talk to him? He's all right."

"Just what Kincaid needs, one of his men bellyaching about mistreatment from the CO," Tim jeered. He hung his head. "I don't know if I can last much longer. I've vowed that under no circumstances will I salute Luther Jones. So far he's been with Kincaid or some of the commissioned officers and I could get away with it by a kind of general salute. It won't last. I've disappeared around corners until I'm sick of it. I don't know any other way to keep from meeting Luther face to face and having to deliberately refuse to answer his salute."

"Golly, I don't know." Yet Sam never stayed stumped for long. His freckled face brightened. "Maybe Grampaw can help. I mean, without using specifics. He musta met up with some officers he couldn't respect when he served in the Spanish-American War."

"Don't get me in any more trouble than I

154

already am," Tim warned and stretched his weary body. The extra duty given as punishment for Luther's so-called infractions took its toll. Tim's mental state demanded even more.

When the men of Dale had bedded down for the night, Sam spoke in the darkness. "Grampaw, you being the oldest and supposedly the wisest of all of us —"

Catcalls drowned him out but nothing deterred Sam once he had an idea in mind. "Hey, you guys, let me finish, will you?"

"Sure, Sammy," someone yelled. "But make it fast. I'm done in." A chorus of agreement followed.

"I just wondered, what if sometime, somewhere, a poor, tired soldier like me — or any of us — meets up with an officer who's a real skunk? S'pose I decide I can't salute that skunk but I don't want to get kicked out of the army. What do I do? Hold my nose and salute anyway?"

Dead silence hung heavy in the barracks. Tim had the feeling every man there knew exactly who Sam meant and why he had asked the question. With the sharpening sense of what was in the hearts and minds of company D, he felt the men's rough sympathy for him and a clear assurance that not one man there would betray him.

Grampaw's drawl cut into Tim's musings. "Well, I found myself in just that position once. Not long ago, in fact. I guess you boys may have expeeeerienced it too." He hung onto the word.

The barracks lay quieter than a reconnaissance team in enemy territory.

"So what did you do?" Sam asked, his voice charged with emotion.

"Just what you said. Now, a man can't tell whether you're lookin' in his eyes if you look at the bridge of his nose square in between." Grampaw's advice hung in the night air. "Every time I meet-uh-met that skunk, I just stare and salute, *not the man, but the uniform he's wearin'*. I reckon our government doesn't always know when a skunk or two sneaks in the service." Grampaw's voice dropped persuasively. "The uniform of an officer in the United States of America stands for a whole lot. For the givin' of life and bravery and never turnin' back. You'll never go wrong if you just remember that. Why, the no-count skunk inside that fancy dress won't ever know the difference, but you will and that's what counts."

"Thanks, Grampaw." Sam's words sounded muffled.

Thanks, Grampaw, Tim's lightened spirits echoed. A triumphant smile erased the perpetual scowl that had occupied his face since Luther arrived in all his unearned glory. Luther never would know the difference: Tim and the men from Dale would salute his officer's uniform, but never the man underneath.

One thing bothered Tim more than all else. He could handle the unfair punishment, the dirty jobs, and the extra work but when Sam reported their new CO had given orders for all mail to be sorted in *his* office, Tim's world turned black.

"I also heard he isn't above *reading* that mail. Says it's up to him to censor anything that might hurt the country." Sam snorted. "Since when has he cared that much about the good old U.S.? I think it's so he can keep track of what you and Miss — you and your wife write back and forth."

"Does Kincaid know?" Tim demanded.

"Yeah, but what can he do? Luther outranks him. Kincaid's walking on eggs for fear the new CO will pull strings and keep him from going across with company D." He looked toward heaven and made a horrible face. "Can you imagine what we'd get if Luther had his pick? Hey, that reminds me. You haven't said anything about hearing from home lately."

Tim's gaze drilled into his friend's anxious face. "We both know why now, don't we? Sam, if I write to Hope and send it in one of your letters would your family deliver it and keep their mouths shut?"

Sam's eyes gleamed. "You bet! Dad's told us never to talk about our business to other folks and to talk about other folks's affairs even less. Write your letter, buddy. I'll see it gets where it's supposed to go." His boyish attitude changed abruptly. "Better do it right away, though. We may not be here much longer."

"Have you heard something?"

Sam grinned tormentingly. "Can't say as I have but Grampaw says we're as ready as we're gonna be and I'll bet my next week's rations Sergeant Kincaid agrees. Notice how he's even slackened off a little? Anyway, go write your letter."

"You don't think Luther will open *your* mail, do you?"

"Why should he?" Sam had never looked more innocent. " 'Sides, I know a way to get mail in and out without Luther seeing it. I cozied up to one of the guys who do mail call, bought him some candy and stuff. I told him there was this girl back home who'd be waiting to get letters and I didn't hanker on having anyone else see them. It's all true. I didn't have to lie. He said not to put my letters in the regular mail but give them to him direct."

"But what about incoming mail?" Tim appreciated the unexpected ally yet didn't trust how far he could go without being caught.

Sam's shrewd gaze reassured him. "I also just happened to mention I didn't cotton to having letters addressed to me examined or censored. As long as he handles the mail, we don't have to worry."

That night Tim wrote to Hope and poured out his heart. If they shipped out soon, tonight was too precious to waste.

11

"Miss Hope, beggin' your pardon, Mrs. Wainwright." Burly Andrew Johnson leaned over the big library desk where Hope sat working. He sent a furtive glance around him and dropped his voice to a whisper. "I have something for you."

Hope's heart settled back in place after its wild leap at being called Mrs. Wainwright. She smiled pleasantly. "A message from Sam?"

"You could say that." He awkwardly took an envelope from his pocket, checked to see that those browsing the shelves on this busy Saturday afternoon paid attention to the books only, and smuggled the envelope under a book Hope held. His honest eyes held compassion and understanding when he added, "My boy's proud to be serving with your husband. He'll do everything he can to help him out — they're real buddies."

A delicate wave of pink filled Hope's cheeks. Did the comment hide a secret meaning? "Thank you, Mr. Johnson. Sam is a fine person and I know Timothy admires him a great deal. He says Sam keeps the morale of every man in Dale from sagging even when things get tough."

Mr. Johnson raised expressive eyebrows and whispered again. "You don't know how tough — yet." The brows met in a heavy frown. "Well, just remember. Anything I can do for you, just holler." He straightened, picked up the large stack of books she offered, and raised his voice to a normal, hearty tone. "I'll be in town for another hour or two. If you want to send a message to Ma or the girls — or anything — I'll drop back by." His twinkling eyes brought an answering smile and a gleam of anticipation to Hope.

"How nice of you! Yes, do stop back. I just may have a note for you to deliver."

The friendly farmer grinned and strode out. Hope heard the cough of his old car when it started then a chug-chug down the street. She glanced at her watch. Grace had gone to the cottage for a list she'd left home that morning but would be right back. When the sprightly white-haired lady swept back in bringing a touch of the frosty outdoors still on her cloak, Hope said, "There's something here you should see, Grace." Her imploring eyes brought her friend to the desk even before undoing her bonnet strings or removing the cloak.

Hope slipped the envelope out so Grace could see it. In Sam's penciled scrawl were clear instructions to his family: PASS THIS ON AND KEEP YOUR LIPS BUTTONED ABOUT IT. SEE IF THERE'S AN ANSWER AND SEND IT TO ME.

"Why —" Grace broke off when Miss Hattie stepped up with books to be checked out. Hope concealed the letter from the sharp eyes that so faithfully copied the best styles. Miss Hattie was busily inspecting Hope's simple pink gown.

"Just as I said, that pink's made up until folks would think it came straight from New Yawk."

Hope laughed as much at the dressmaker's ill-concealed pride as at her high-toned way of speaking. Genuine affection shone in her dancing eyes. "Now, Miss Hattie, pride goeth before a fall."

"Hmph! I believe that's *pride goeth before destruction and a haughty spirit before a fall*★," the spirited lady retorted. "Besides, I don't see that the good Lord minds us being glad for the talents He went and gave us. Unless

★ Proverbs 16:18(KJV)

we get too biggety and forget where that talent came from," she conceded. "Never could see no sense in being mealy-mouthed and acting as helpless as newborn kittens." She abruptly turned to Grace who stood smiling at the exchange.

"Would you like a kitten? That old cat of yours must be getting pretty old. My cat died, leaving a litter."

"Thanks, but I don't care to take on an orphan," Grace said.

Miss Hattie straightened her hat until it sat squarely on her head. "Well, I'll see if I can find homes for them. I can keep two but not six. Now if I had a farm, it'd be different." She sighed and her kind old eyes turned misty. "It's about more than a body can bear to see such cunning little creatures have to die before they even get a chance to live."

Tenderhearted Hope impulsively told her, "Miss Hattie, maybe the Johnsons would take the kittens. Mr. Johnson came in earlier and will be back soon. I can ask about the kittens, if you like. With his big barn a few extra cats to catch mice may be welcome."

"You're a sweet child." Miss Hattie patted Hope's hand with her lace-mitted one and gathered her books. "Now, don't forget. Tell him to stop by."

"I will." Hope walked to the library door with her and noticed how happily the woman marched back down the street.

"Run over home and read your letter," Grace advised in a low tone. "I'll watch the library. Take time to answer too."

Hope's slippered feet barely skimmed the worn path between the library and cottage. Its quiet charm enveloped her as usual when she stepped inside. Straight to the desk she flew, dropping the envelope in her haste to get the letter out.

Much later she slipped to her knees, suffering with Timothy and the men of Dale who were under Luther Jones's cruel tyranny. Although Tim said little except that fate, he suspected with much help, had landed Luther in the position of CO, misery and dread over what the future held was written between the lines. Too distressed to pray, Hope simply stayed on her knees and let her Heavenly Father's peace touch her heart until she felt strong enough to take up a pen and reply.

She reread Timothy's final words, her hands still visibly shaking.

I don't know when I will be able to write again at such great length. Rumors are flying that we will be shipped out any moment. Once on the seas, it may be impossible to use Sam's letters as a cover to write to you.

Even in the short time since we arranged this, my mind has worked to our advantage. Already Luther may have intercepted letters. If we stop writing openly, he will grow suspicious and perhaps track down our line of communication. While the idea of him seeing even one word of your messages to me is appalling, we need to keep up a pretense. Write as usual. Fill in the letters with what you're doing, town news, and so on. Then, dearest, write other letters and send them through the Johnsons. They are wonderful, trusted friends who know more of the situation than I have ever told them.

I will also write. Luther won't think it strange that I don't go into detail due to the secrecy of the movements we may make. Remember, every time I simply sign those decoy letters with love, you can know (if they do get through) I am really sending all of my heart.

Already home and you seem far away. Yet I can carry the precious knowledge that you are Mrs. Timothy Wainwright with me.

Hope, my darling, I am trying hard not to let the hatred and bitterness I feel over God letting Luther command us tear my spirit. I am trying to pray. I can't accept Jesus until I know I can do it with a clean heart. Just knowing you are praying for me helps more than I can say.

I love you now and forever,

Timothy

With a prayer for guidance she began to write. Page after page drifted unheeded to the floor. She ended with these words, the contents of her soul exposed on paper.

Go into battle with a cry for God's companionship at all times. Never forget the meaning of your name, Timothy, *honoring God.* There may be mountains and valleys to cross, obstacles higher than your hills of Hope. Yet, our Heavenly Father will be with you — if you invite Him.

She signed the tear-stained letter, quickly put it in an envelope and sealed it, and wrote "Tim" on the outside. A few moments later, eyes bathed in cold water and calmed by time spent alone with God, Hope went back to the library.

Andrew Johnson stood just inside, evidently chatting with Grace. "Why, it's not a mite of trouble. We're just glad there's something we can do to make things easier for Miss Hope and Tim. You know he's been like one of our own for years. I don't feel sneaking mean, either. If that Justin Farrell. . . ." He wheeled and snapped his lips shut.

Hope fearfully looked around the library. Surely Mr. Johnson wouldn't be talking like this in front of others! She breathed a sigh of relief when Aunt Grace asked, "Is your letter ready?"

"Oh, yes." She thrust it into Mr. Johnson's big hand. "I'm sorry to keep you."

"I just came in, but I s'pose I'd better get along. Ma said take whatever time I needed but not a minute more. Ain't that just like her?" His sheepish smile gave way that he wouldn't change her for anything.

"Oh, Mr. Johnson." Hope caught his sleeve when he turned to go out. "Miss Hattie's got four orphan kittens she can't care for. Would you let them live on your farm?"

His broad face beamed. "No reason not to. I always did hanker after motherless critters." He shook her hand vigorously and closed the door behind him.

"Suppertime." Aunt Grace turned her window sign to CLOSED. "I can't wait five minutes more to hear what's happened."

Safely inside the cottage sanctuary, Hope told her. Dismayed at the news, Aunt Grace rocked and nodded while Hope's nimble fingers sorted letter pages and read bits here and there.

When she had made sense of the torrent of explanations, Grace nodded again and the dismay changed to satisfaction. "Hope, you've prayed and prayed for Timothy. God sometimes has what we think are mighty strange paths to bring His children back where they belong, to Him. Instead of moaning about Luther, let's just start trusting God a little more. These trials and tribulations may be His way of bringing Timothy to the point where the only option he has is to turn to Jesus."

Hope refolded her priceless letter and slipped the envelope into the cleverly concealed pocket of Miss Hattie's pink creation. "I know."

"How much are you willing to let God do if it means Timothy's salvation?"

Dry-eyed, Hope stared at Grace and mutely shook her head.

"You might ask yourself that." Grace stood. "Now, we have a job to do so let's get our supper over with so we can get started on it. Having the library open Saturdays after supper means work."

The men, women, children, and young people who trooped in for books that evening offered a respite from Hope's chaotic thoughts. Grace closed the doors promptly at eight o'clock with the remark, "Folks are sure reading a lot these days! That's good. There's no excuse to be ignorant or uninformed."

Hope caught the proud way her friend surveyed the well-stocked shelves. Small as the Dale library was, it still held an immense variety and Hope often marveled how Grace could manage to interest the community, and keep ahead of that interest! Yet in between Hope's numerous tasks had run Grace's compelling question: *How much are you willing to let God do if it means Timothy's salvation?*

Days later Hope answered in the way she knew she must, but only after soul searching. No matter what it took, she would accept it — for Jesus' sake, and Tim's.

In spite of the rumors, company D did not ship out immediately. October drizzled its way into November. Letters arrived with a certain regularity. Hope kept each one and read it until she knew the words by heart. Those that straggled through after having been opened for "inspection" occupied a lesser place in Hope's heart. How hard to write naturally while knowing unfriendly eyes might read the message! But the letters that came via smiling Mr. Johnson, or from one of his family, outshone diamonds and rubies.

What did a shortage of sugar matter? Or meatless Tuesdays and a dozen other small sacrifices? God still controlled the world and Hope rejoiced through her fears. She hadn't realized how much the war matured even the young until Maura's visit. Aunt Grace tactfully excused herself so the two might chat freely.

"Hope, ye have always been a pretty colleen but now your eyes show understandin' and ye are no longer a child." Maura's Irish-blue eyes looked deeper than ever. "If himself could just forget his position." Worry wrinkled her face. "Sometimes he's for bein' so brittle it's a wonder a finger doesn't snap off when touched."

"Does he hear from Luther often?"

Maura snorted matter of factly. "Not so ye'd be noticin' it. A few lines here and there." She pursed her lips, glanced at the clock, and reluctantly rose. "I have bread to set. Child, for ye'll always be that to me, I can't help believing that one day everything will work out for good. Himself took a wrong turn somewhere and got too big for his breeches. God knows what it will take to set him straight." The wisdom of years rested in her voice and gave it authority. "That's one of the reasons I stay on. Someday Justin Farrell will need someone."

Hope had little faith in premonitions yet Maura's words sent a chill through her. "I just hope he forgives me."

Maura paused in gathering her warm cloak around her and opened her eyes wide in surprise. "But don't ye see, lamb, it's himself he has to be forgivin' first, for whatever it is that's inside." She left and Hope pondered what she meant but came to no conclusion. The idea of Justin Farrell having a hidden sin or regret tilted the very pedestal on which Dale had placed him!

Grace Forsythe wisely supplied her lending library with a variety of newspapers and magazines as well as books. With Everett and Seattle so close, she saw no reason not to take advantage of their culture while still enjoying Dale's isolation. She and Hope often debated the issues of the day. Suffragettes, prohibitionists, and war correspondents vied for front page space. Both agreed women not only should but must have the right to vote.

Grace became highly incensed at those who laughed at the idea. "For almost forty years amendments to the Constitution have been proposed and introduced in Congress, one after another." Her eyes sparkled like sapphires. "It's only a matter of time until it becomes law. I'm just sorry it hasn't been passed. I would like to have voted for Mr. Wilson."

On Prohibition she wasn't so strong. "I hate Demon Rum," she said. "But I'm not sure, especially with this war going on, how and where we'd get the men to enforce it." She puffed out her cheeks and tried to look pompous. "Of course, they could empower women."

Hope couldn't help laughing at the idea. "Well, it's been proposed for nearly a year. By the time enough states ratify it, if they ever do, the war may be over. Anyway, it says here Prohibition wouldn't take effect for a whole year after it becomes law." She thought of Luther's sickening breath and disgusting actions when he'd been drinking. "Why would anyone want to drink? It's repulsive."

"I agree. Alcohol is good in cleaning wounds but should be kept for people's outsides, not their insides.

"Hope, I know your father was very much against it but now that you are in control of your life and out of his home, have you thought any more about training to be a nurse?"

"Yes, I have." Her amber eyes darkened. "I just feel I need to do more than I now am."

"Good. The local chapter is looking for more recruits for the volunteer nurses' aides. I took the liberty of mentioning your name as a possible helper. Someone should contact you soon."

"What will I have to do? What about my library work?" Hope wanted to know. "I can't just live with you and not earn my keep."

"Don't be a ninny. This is wartime. If you are needed elsewhere, don't hesitate to prepare." Her keen gaze cut through Hope's attempt to sort things out. "Who knows? You might even be useful overseas with the Red Cross if you're trained and ready."

"What kind of training is required?" Hope eagerly asked.

"I understand that you'll be given some kind of elementary hygiene course and most likely some home nursing training. It won't be a complete training course in nursing but enough so you can assist. Or would you want to take a full nursing course? It would require more time and hard work but since you've been here with me, I know neither of those is an obstacle."

Hope considered for a long moment. "I-I don't know if I'd be a good nurse. Perhaps I should fulfill the volunteer nurses' aide requirements first and if the war continues longer than we expect, I can decide later about more training." She stared into the shadows even the bright blaze from a merry little fire in the fireplace couldn't dispel.

"One thing this war has done is to abolish some of the prejudice against nursing as a profession," Grace remarked. Her fingers never missed a stitch of the khaki-colored wool sweater that rapidly formed on her shining steel needles.

Hope bent her head over the heavy wristlet she had nearly completed. "I know. Some of the so-called best families have daughters proudly wearing uniforms." She sighed. "I wonder if even that will convince Father there can be honor in helping others, even when some of the tasks are hard and what he calls demeaning."

But for once Justin Farrell's prejudices seemed pathetically insignificant. The vivid image of Timothy lying in a Red Cross hut somewhere silenced her and overcame fear of her own inadequacy. She wouldn't wait for the local chapter representative to call. If more volunteers were needed to care for young men like Timothy and Sam, she would get ready for duty.

The next morning Hope signed the necessary forms and became part of the vast organization dedicated to helping those in need at home and abroad. When she firmly crossed the *t* at the end of her signature, Hope Wainwright felt she too had crossed — over to the challenge of a lifetime.

12

Timothy had asked Sam to spread the word he didn't want any more Camp Lewis occupants than necessary to know Luther was Tim's stepbrother. The men of Dale backed him all the way, frequently commiserating with him on the new CO's latest exercise in cruelty. This loyalty helped Tim through the worst job and the meanest punishment. He set his jaw, saluted the uniform that housed Luther, and kept his own counsel. Only to Sam did he let out his anger and hatred. The habit of aloneness that began in Dale couldn't be broken completely and, to some extent, Tim remained a loner.

Every new feat brought a furtive grin to Sergeant Kincaid's seamed face and a scowl to Luther's handsome features. The sergeant never lost an opportunity to praise company D and he always added, "This is what you get when I take a bunch of small town boys and farmers and train them." But the men who respected him always caught the twinkle lurking in back of his steely eyes.

Hope's regular letters also sustained and encouraged Tim. When he saw evidence of tampering, and then noticed the untouched condition of his friends' mail, his face grew grim. Someday the long overdue reckoning would come between him and Luther and when it did . . . at this point he always switched to another thought. He memorized the clandestine letters and tore them to bits, despising Luther even more when he did so. He learned to love Sam as the brother he never had and went so far as to discuss with him some of his dreams after the war.

"I don't care about a mansion," he said slowly one afternoon when the gray sky wept and the trees moaned. "I know I'll be a good teacher. Hope won't mind not having all the possessions Justin provided. I'm saving every bit of pay I can and sending it home to her. Grace Forsythe won't hear of Hope paying board so Hope is stashing it away. Not in her father's bank, either, as you know!"

"I'm sending most of my pay home too," Sam told him confidentially. "Dad's going to make me a full partner on the farm. I love animals and digging in the earth and seeing things grow." He sighed, strangely wistful.

"Wish this would be over so we could get started."

"Yeah, but the news from the front is anything but good." Tim closed his eyes. Newspaper headlines proclaiming new losses for the Allies affected him more profoundly than he cared to admit. "Now that ice and snow have stopped the fighting at Ypres, even if Britain can break through the Siegfried line with tanks, they don't have the troops to follow up."

"I know and I don't see how London and the other English cities can take the bombing from the zeppelins." He bit his lip. "I know it's selfish, but I thank God every day those bombs aren't falling on America." His voice quivered then hardened to tempered steel. "That's one of the reasons why we have to go over, so that bombs won't fall on my Dale."

Tim gripped his friend's strong hand but didn't reply.

Much of the good-natured banter had stilled in the barracks and only Sam's clowning could bring genuine laughter. Two days later Sergeant Kincaid marched in and ordered, "Ten-shun!"

Soldiers scrambled from their bunks and onto their feet with sharp salutes.

"At ease," Kincaid barked. The biggest

grin the men had ever seen on his face spread. "We're shipping out. Tomorrow."

A moment of stunned silence gave in to a cacophony of cheers. The long weeks of waiting exploded; pandemonium raged. The men of Dale, now welded into a fighting unit, stood ready.

Sam put the icing on the cake. Rounding his expressive eyes into false awe, he waited until the cheering subsided and innocently asked, "Did the Kaiser send us a personal invitation? Just think, buddies, we're gonna see France, beyoo-tiful France with all those French people just waiting for us to come."

Sergeant Kincaid cut short his nonsense with a sour pretense that fooled no one. "You'll be happy to know, Johnson, I'm going right along with all of you." He snorted and became again icicle Kincaid. "Any man who sloughs off in my outfit answers to me and he won't like what happens."

Grampaw voiced the uppermost question in Timothy's mind. He cocked his head to one side. "Sarge, who's gonna be our CO over there? Seems to me our present Commanding Officer's so valuable here he can't be spared."

A blanket of quiet descended. Sergeant Kincaid slowly straightened to full height.

"Same CO." He snapped a salute to his men, turned on his heel, and marched out.

"Well, life ain't all fried chicken and strawberry shortcake," Grampaw observed to no one in particular. "Leastways we've got Kincaid."

A solid murmur of approval lifted a bit of Tim's apprehension. He'd prayed for days that Luther would be left behind but the thorn in his side remained. As Grampaw said, things could have been worse if Sergeant Kincaid had been reassigned.

"Boys, get your gear together and write your letters home," Grampaw directed. "The seagulls won't be delivering any messages and I never heard much about post offices in France."

Timothy made short work of his packing. Then he wrote two notes, mailed one, and unobtrusively slipped the other to Sam who still laboriously wrote in his distinctive scrawl. Tim stepped out into the early winter evening and gazed around. Wisps of fog still hung and softened the bleak parade grounds and barracks. Nostalgia filled Tim: At least Camp Lewis had felt close to Dale. Mount Rainier with its ever-white crown lay to the east and a little south. North and east, Dale was crouched in its green valley, protected by the hills of home. Would he ever see the hills of Hope again? Or would he become one of too many fighting men whose bodies lay in unmarked graves far from everything they loved?

He could not, he would not, desert. Yet for the space of a single heartbeat Timothy Wainwright longed to run. Shaken by the storm of emotion that rocked him, he silently cried for help. *God, if You are real. . . .* He couldn't go on. Head bowed in despair, a few words from the first letter Hope had sent through the Johnsons crept into his soul.

Go into battle with a cry for God's companionship at all times . . . Our Heavenly Father will be with you — if you invite Him.

Did he dare? Timothy shivered in the dank night. On the other hand, did he dare go across without God? Closer to the point of reaching out than ever before in his life, Tim's inner struggle dissolved when a crude oath in a familiar voice sliced the darkness. *Luther!*

The moment of feeling God calling to him evaporated and Tim wearily went back to his barracks to wait for morning and the beginning of a new world.

Later the men of Dale pieced together the horror of their crossing. Some had never even seen the Pacific Ocean; others who had still faced the wild Atlantic unprepared. Late November and early December storms attacked the troop ship until Tim, Sam, and the others often wondered if it would break apart on the heaving seas. Appalling conditions from overcrowding and poor food joined to enervate even the hardiest. Those who had faced wild animals in the forest, danger from falling trees, and a multitude of other adverse circumstances fell helpless prey to the elements. Most of the men suffered seasickness until they wondered if they'd die; some prayed aloud that they would.

Tim miraculously escaped but spent day and night caring for Grampaw, Sam, and his friends. With so much sickness in such cramped quarters, fresh air became an unreachable luxury. No amount of cleaning could rid the below-deck area of the stench.

During it all, Commanding Officer Luther Jones and a few of his cohorts enjoyed the best of food, freedom to walk the decks, and clean sleeping quarters. Tim suspected Luther had bribed the sullen captain of the ship. The few times Tim saw Luther, he held his head high, looked straight at the bridge of the CO's nose, and saluted the immaculate uniform so out of place on this wretched vessel.

By the time they landed, less than half the men were in fighting condition. They were put in lorries and jolted over shell-torn roads. A farmhouse had been commandeered for the officers. The enlisted and drafted men were herded to a barn where a leaking roof and filthy straw over dried cow dung offered no more than partial shelter from the elements. For hours Timothy listened to the retching of still-sick comrades and the cries from those who uneasily slept. At last he could bear no more. Wrapping himself in a none-too-clean blanket, he crept outside.

A minute later Sam joined him. Hollow-eyed, he looked little like the laughing friend Tim knew. "Listen to that," he hissed.

Tim threw his head back. Music and laughter from the old farmhouse and the pounding sounds of dancing resounded in the night air.

"Dancing, with us out here freezing and sick! Luther Jones had better never be in the front lines of battle. The grapevine has it that not all dead officers in France are being killed by the Huns — at least those skunks wearing the uniform."

A thrill of horror shot through Tim. "You mean —"

"I just mean that if I were Luther Jones I'd

be mighty sure to keep back from the places where a man can get killed." Sam laughed harshly but kept his voice low. "I doubt we have to worry about it. All the pretty ribbons can't hide a coward."

"Let's see if we can find a place to get a little sleep." Tim didn't want to talk about Luther. He looked up. The rain had stopped but trees still dripped. A few steady stars poked through the heavy cloud cover. Off to one side an open hut looked strangely inviting. The two soldiers quietly considered it. "Bah, as dirty as the barn," Tim said but Sam whispered, "At least not as crowded. Here, put down your blanket to keep us out of the muck. We'll pull mine over us."

Incredibly, they slept. Tim opened his eyes to a murky dawn with renewed strength from even the few hours of rest. Sam looked better too. A stubble of fuzz couldn't hide the lines in his face but the darkest of the circles under his eyes had vanished.

The France Sam predicted an eternity ago would be waiting for them never materialized. Trench after trench, mile after mile of French countryside all to gain at a terrible cost what seemed inches blurred into days, weeks, and months. Christmas passed with a feeble attempt at celebration — a few candle stubs. Letters and packages from home that survived the journey were gladly shared along with hot coffee and doughnuts from a Red Cross hut sent in a field ambulance. The cheering men from Dale swallowed hard and refused to dwell on memories of Christmas at home.

Neither Tim nor Sam received word from Dale. Sam glumly said, "To think I skipped out on the Christmas Eve service last year. What I'd give to be there now." He licked a final doughnut crumb from his fingers. "The birth of Jesus and all His teachings about peace sure don't match this place."

"Sam." Tim suddenly felt he had to know. "You, I mean, are you a Christian?" He managed a laugh. "We've never really talked about it. I know you go to church and everything, but —"

"I'm a Christian. Don't see how a fella could stand it over here if he wasn't." He waited a minute. "I always wished I could tell you about it but you never seemed interested."

Tim asked curiously, "Then why did you miss last year's service?"

Sam's ears turned red. "Aw, I had an argument with Dad and up and said I wasn't going. Then I was too proud to back down. Never felt worse in my life, until now." He almost whispered the last words.

"Hope wants me to accept Jesus. Sometimes I even want to and not just for her. But what kind of a God is it who lets folks like Justin Farrell and Luther Jones run the world?"

"You don't think *they're* Christians, do you? My dog's a better Christian than either of them." Sam's eyes flashed scornfully.

"Justin never misses church," Tim protested. "He's head of a dozen committees and Reverend Slater jumps when Justin gives the word."

"Going to church and being on committees doesn't get you to heaven or anywhere else . . . you just end up looking good in front of others." Sam made the most of his opportunity. "The trouble with most folks when they're trying to find God is that they look in the wrong places. Like when you go fishing. Now, the city slickers come out to Dale and go down to the river then complain 'cause the fish ain't biting. *We* know if you want fish, you don't go out in the open where the river runs bold as day for everyone to see. You look in the quiet, more hidden places." He stretched and yawned.

"The way I see it, God's to be found in the quiet people like my folks and Grace Forsythe and Miss Hattie and Hope Far—, I mean, Hope Wainwright."

Another snatch of conversation settled into Tim's mind. "That's what Grace said." He thought hard to remember her exact words. "She told me not to judge God by those who claim to know Him, but by those who do."

"Golly, she sure can put things clear!" Admiration lit Sam's tired face. "Like we can either judge the army by what we know of our dear CO or by Sergeant Kincaid." He sat bolt upright. "You have to admit, he's stuck with us. I heard him telling Luther what his men got, he would too. He got us out of that stinking barn in a hurry!"

They fell quiet and Tim's grin matched Sam's, remembering the outraged sergeant who had bypassed Luther and gone straight to the highest ranking officer he could find on behalf of company D. But Tim's mind quickly went back to their earlier conversation.

"Do you ever feel like God's real close to you? Hope said something about that."

"Tim, even out here on this battlefield, in between the cannon fire and yelling and dying, I feel God's presence." A kind of glory made Sam's freckled face beautiful in the dim light. "You can, too, if you'll accept His Son."

Tim felt his heart being pulled in two. "I'd give anything on earth — even Hope — to be able to feel that," he cried. "I can't do it, Sam. I'd be a hypocrite. The way I hate Luther, how can I expect God to listen to me?"

Two strong arms shot out and fastened themselves to Tim's shoulders. "Listen to me, Timothy Wainwright!" Sam's brown eyes blazed. "Who do you think Jesus came for anyway? Wonderful people like my folks and Hope and Grace? Oh, sure, He did come for them but not because they were wonderful. Jesus came because people are *sinners.* He said so Himself, that He didn't come because of the righteous any more than our doctors and medics waste time on us when we're well. Jesus came to save poor, miserable soldiers like you and me — and He doesn't want us to wait until we can somehow make ourselves good enough, which we can't anyway, before we come to Him."

Sam stopped for breath and his hands fell to his sides. "Tim, buddy, God wants you *now,* just the way you are."

"If only I could believe that!" Tim's low cry of agony reached only Sam's ears, and God's.

In an entirely different tone of voice, Sam quietly said, "God says it in the Bible. So does Jesus. If we can't believe God's Word, what *can* we believe?"

Tim leaped to his feet and plunged into

the darkness. Still mindful of possible danger surrounding him, he cautiously wormed his way to the blackest spot he could find without leaving the vicinity. Home, Hope, Sam, God, Luther, Justin, all blended into the greatest need of human-kind — the need for God to fill an emptiness nothing else could satisfy.

"God, if You are there, speak to me. I can't go on without You." Tim could barely hear his own words. Over and over they pounded in his brain, as relentless as the sounds of battle that never ceased except to prepare for something even worse.

My son, I love you.

Who had spoken? Tim wildly looked around, feeling that someone stood near yet unable to see anyone. He pivoted in place and searched out every clinging shadow, his eyes now accustomed to the darkness re-lieved by a few pale stars.

Realization came. The Presence he felt must be Sam's God. The voice must be in his heart or soul or mind. For a traitorous moment he wondered if he were going crazy or had been shellshocked. He'd read of such things happening in battle and company D had been fighting for a long time.

A snap of the fingers later he knew better. A feeling of calmness and peace like nothing he had ever known surrounded his cold, trembling body, similar to his mother's warm, loving arms.

The war, Luther, and Justin receded.

Timothy Wainwright stood alone in the night. No, not alone. The Savior of the world had gently come into Tim's heart at his unspoken invitation.

13

On a lonely stretch of ground in France, under cover of distant fire, Timothy Wainwright and Sam Johnson whispered in the night. Too tired by the constant demands on their already over-worked bodies to sleep, they spoke of home, friends, and Tim's conversion — but no longer of the future. Anything other than continuing war faded into a distant dream, too nebulous to hold in the face of fighting.

Tim's right hand lay inside his shirt and clutched the worn New Testament and remnants of the last letter he had received from Hope dated weeks before. Time meant nothing here except when he related events from the date of the letter.

Something in the air, an uneasy warning that chilled men's souls, settled over company D, silencing even Sam's wit. He clutched his weapon and peered into the gloom. "Seems like nights should be getting shorter," he muttered. "We're months into 1918. At least it's warmer."

"We can be glad for that. If I get home I'm never going to be cold again." Memory of the weeks of fighting made Tim shiver.

"Tim." Sam inched a little closer. "You said *if* you get home, not *when*. Don't you think we'll make it?" Desolation filled Sam's question. "Forget it. Of course you'll get home. Me, too, and Grampaw and the others —"

Tim knew in a flash his comrade was picturing the broken bodies carried back from the front lines by medics and the blanketed forms, some from Dale, some that would go home to grieving families. "Most of us are still alive, thanks to Sergeant Kincaid's training."

"Tad Wilson got shipped home, Dad said in his last letter." Sam changed position a bit. "He's pretty badly shot up but the doctors say he's going to make it. You know Tad. No one can keep him down for long."

Something warm and wet splashed on Tim's hand. He hadn't known he could still cry. "Why are we here anyway?" he whispered fiercely. "Why should boys like Tad and men like Grampaw and the rest of us care so much about this country when it isn't ours?" Yet his rebellion died immediately. "Sorry. It's just that sometimes nothing seems real." He passed a weary hand over his eyes and lightened his voice while keeping it low. "Sam, there's something I want to say then I'll never talk about it again." He took a deep breath, held it, then slowly breathed out. "Until I came over here I blamed God for all my troubles. If anything happens, I want you to know — and tell Hope — I know God planned it so you'd be here with me." He ignored his friend's gasp and continued. "Ever since I told God I couldn't go on without Him, things with Luther have been even worse although I try to keep out of his way. I know he must be intercepting Hope's letters. We both know your letters have been opened too. That has to be why I never hear. I keep writing to her, even though I know they probably aren't getting mailed.

"Anyway, having you here to keep reminding me that God loves me and is allowing me to suffer makes the difference. Don't get me wrong. God isn't making Luther act the way he does; the devil's good at that. I guess I'm just saying thanks, buddy — thanks for all the times you show me something in the Bible that fits what we're going through and for never letting your own faith waver, even when mine does." He groped in the darkness until he found Sam's hand and closed his strong fingers around it.

Sam lay quiet for a long time. Then he choked out, "You think *I'm* a witness to *you?* Tim Wainwright, I've wanted to give up a dozen times rather than keep fighting when I'm so tired I could die. I never would have made it this long if you hadn't been here."

A moment more they silently lay in the trench then in a twinkling a roar such as even the fiercest battle brought shook them. Sam shouted, leaped to his feet, rifle ready — and fell.

"God, help!" With superhuman strength Tim sprang to his friend's side and hoisted him on his shoulders. With the same dead run that once carried him to victory on the athletic field, he sprinted back from the thunder of a battlefield gone mad. *"Medic! Medic!"*

"Here." Strong hands relieved Tim of his burden.

"Is he alive?" Tim's heart skipped and waited for a reply.

"Yes, but we have to get him to the field hospital." Before he finished speaking the man had beckoned help by the flare of cannon fire.

Tim readied his own weapon and raced back to the trench, renewed by his hatred of the German army. Sam's earnest freckled face never left him as Tim's sweaty hands opened and closed around his trusty weapon. Every trace of fatigue fled before the need ahead.

The rest of the night, all the next day and night, and for three days and nights following the battle raged, the worst company D had experienced. Men fell asleep on their feet, regained consciousness, and fought on. Bandaged, bloody, and determined, they stubbornly held their own against a force three times as large and powerful. Grampaw had once predicted how the men of Dale would perform under fire. Now his prediction came gloriously true. A wounded but unbowed Sergeant Kincaid fought with them, jaw set, eyes straight ahead.

A lifetime ago when the world was still sane Sam had quipped, "D for Dale, Kincaid to aid." Every time Tim thought of it his lips tightened and he forced himself to put worry over Sam aside. War left no room for personal feelings when duty called. Only in the brief rest he took when his body would not be denied and when Sergeant Kincaid ordered him to sleep permitted snatches of other thoughts. Chief among them was the pounding certainty that Sam would see Hope the minute the military agreed. By concentrating on and holding close to the idea, a little comfort came.

One good thing came from the terrible days and nights: Commanding Officer Luther Jones put away his arrogance and buried any trace of cowardice. He fought side by side with the same privates he'd bossed and made miserable only days before. Luther stayed away from the area where Tim lay; when they moved up, one forged ahead on the left, one on the right, but neither turned back. Deep in his heart, Tim found himself glad — not just for Justin's sake, but for Luther's. Tim had never quite been able to forget Sam's face when he talked about officers who didn't come home, and not all from German fire.

A grudging respect toward the now-disheveled, grimy-faced CO became clear when Grampaw admitted in a rare lull, "Guess bein' with us may have rubbed off some."

Tim noticed Luther's ears perk up and his face turn a dull red even when his lips twitched in a grin.

When that particular battle ended, an inevitable letdown followed but only for a few hours until new orders came for them to proceed. A certain strip must be taken, a piece of terrain vitally important to the success of the Allied campaign. Under cover of darkness they stole forward, positioned themselves, and waited for reinforcements already on their way. At midnight word came: The entire company had been annihilated and company D lay in danger of being cut off.

"Fall back!" The order passed from man to man. Muttered curses and pounding footsteps accompanied the retreat. Even the bravest hearts quailed. Marching toward the enemy was one thing; being surrounded with no means of escape posed far more serious problems.

Five minutes later lurid red light bathed the battlefield as a barrage of machine gun fire, the boom of cannons, and a spate of rifle fire took center stage. Tim shuddered and took cover at Sergeant Kincaid's order, yet little protection could be found against the holocaust. Men and machines looked bathed in blood. Tim's mouth went dry. It must be the end of the world. Yet he fought on until the enemy gradually gave way. Were they unaware of their superior strength? Had the determination of the smaller band convinced them to continue would be disastrous? Was it a trick?

"Get outta here, men!" Sergeant Kincaid ordered. Soldiers on both sides of Tim stumbled to their feet and lurched into the welcome darkness so in contrast with the

197

terrible red. One by one they disappeared, many too shocked to do more than follow orders.

Tim hesitated, shut his eyes tight to adjust them to the gloom of night, and started back. Someone brushed against him and he stiffened.

"C'mon, son," Grampaw whispered. The eerie silence stung Tim's ears the way the smell of gunpowder stung his nose and eyes. The older man vanished after the others.

Tim took one step then a second. Something halted him. A sound? A feeling? A kind of presence?

He shook his head. Once in what felt like another world he had felt the Presence of God but it hadn't been what he now experienced. Why did his feet feel riveted to the ground?

"Timothy."

A breath of cool air flitted against his hot face. He strained to hear. Hallucinations came all too often in battle. Why should he hear voices when the rest of the company had dragged, run, or been carried back from the front?

"Timothy."

"God, is it You? Did the enemy get me?" Strange. When he thought about dying, it hadn't been like this — standing on a deserted battlefield alone and hearing God's voice.

"Timothy. Help."

The soldier in him bounded to the forefront and rudely shoved aside mental confusion. No voice of God asked for help. Someone needed him.

The strangest search of his life began. On hands and knees, Timothy Wainwright crawled from trench to trench in the black night. Heavy rain fell and covered the slight sounds he made. He checked every fallen soldier for the slightest sign of life but without success. The crumpled bodies strewn in grotesque positions where they had fallen made him nauseous but still he persisted. The roar of a hundred now-silent guns drummed in his ear. Yet now and then that faint call, *"Timothy, help,"* beckoned as an oasis lures desert travelers.

If only he could hold the night, he thought in despair. Soon dawn would creep over the scene of carnage and ruthlessly expose his scant cover. A single living, moving being offered the perfect target. Then the voice came no more. Whoever had called probably lay dead of blood loss, his lips silenced forever.

Tim listened while lying flat at the foot of a small rise. A minute passed, almost a lifetime. Not even the song of a bird broke the ominous stillness. Surely none of the men would have climbed the hill, or if one had, enemy fire had picked him off. Even now the enemy could be lying in wait beyond that fragile barrier.

At this life or death crossroads Tim sighed and faced back. Then a power beyond himself turned him around. He could not retreat without completing his quest and examining what lay over the little hill.

Slowly, carefully, he bellied his way up and looked over. A single streak of dawn outlined the huddled form on the other side, a man whose suffering eyes and cracked lips cried out for help.

Tim clapped his hands over his mouth to keep from screaming. His muscles tightened. Great beads of sweat coated his gray face and an icy chill enveloped him. The man who lay below him, felled by the Huns, was Luther Jones.

Savage, unbridled joy burst inside Tim. The moment of reckoning had come, the time he had planned for and anticipated in all the years of merciless torment since Luther came to Dale. A cruel smile formed on Tim's lips and he threw his head back, looked directly into Luther's eyes, and shifted his body to creep back over the other side of the rise. What more fitting punishment than to leave Luther to the Germans?

"*No!*" A great sob tore out of Tim's soul. If the God of heaven and earth could send His Son to die for sinners, how could he who had accepted Jesus harbor this sickening desire for revenge? "God, forgive me." Regardless of possible watching eyes, Tim heaved himself over the hill and slid down beside his stepbrother.

"I prayed that you'd come," Luther croaked.

Tim had to bend close to hear the words that fell from Luther's swollen, parched lips. He grabbed for his canteen, held Luther's bloodstreaked head up, and waited until he drank his fill.

"Where are you hurt?" Tim demanded and anxiously eyed the growing light in the east.

"Broken ankle. Didn't dare try and go back so I played dead."

"We have to get out of here before it's light and they come to see why we stopped firing." Tim ran practiced hands over Luther's body, relieved to discover that except for the cut on his head that had bled freely and the ankle he appeared to be all right. Even as he spoke, the sound of guns greeted the new day.

"Go without me." Luther turned his head away. "We can't make it with this ankle. Tell them at home that I —"

"Don't be a fool!" Tim glared into Luther's face. "Think I'd dare go back to Dale without you?" Some of Tim's old bitterness crept into his voice. "Justin Farrell would run me out of town."

Luther grunted. "Is that why you came? I don't think so."

"There isn't time to talk about it now. We've got to get over that hill." Tim grimly bundled Luther across his back in the carry hold he'd used to bring in a deer back home. With surprising strength he got them back up the rise, over the other side, and well on their way back from the front before staggering to a stop near a small grove of trees. "Have to rest," he gasped. He felt a wrench at his shoulder when he lowered Luther to the ground.

The next minute he was looking down straight into the barrel of his rifle. Before he could fully comprehend the situation, Luther ordered in a deadly voice, "Swear by the God I hear you've accepted that you won't leave me, no matter what happens!" His haggard face twitched.

Tim flung himself on Luther and clawed at the weapon. He wrested the rifle from the weaker man and pinned Luther's arms to the uneven ground beneath them. "That's fever talking, not you. We're going all the way and we're going together — unless the Huns get us on the way."

The fight left Luther. Shame, hope, and desire kindled in his face. "Do you mean that? After everything?"

"I do." Tim released Luther and crossed his arms before him. "I'm not going anywhere without you. Do we go or stay here and argue until the Germans come?"

"If you'll get off me, we'll go." The glimmer of a real smile on lips that so often sneered brought an answering gleam to Tim's dark eyes. He got up and helped Luther to a sitting position. Then he examined the twisted foot, poking and pushing until Luther growled and asked if he thought he was a medic.

"Are you sure it's broken?" Tim demanded.

"Yeah. Felt a bone snap. Splint it if you can. Otherwise it will have to go as is," Luther ordered with some of his old arrogance.

"Yes, sir." But Timothy laughed when he said it and went to search for a sturdy stick. A downed tree limb did the trick and soon the two stood, Luther using a stout branch for a rude crutch.

"Which way, Columbus? I'm not so clear-headed. Can't lead an expedition," he mumbled.

Tim shot an anxious glance at the signs of fever evident in Luther's face. "By now we may be cut off. Can't go ahead, that's for certain. If we aren't able to go ahead or back. . . ." A sudden thought released some of the tension in his body. "Luther, remember how hunters from Dale sometimes got caught out in unexpected storms? Looks to me like the best thing we can do is stay right here." His keen gaze scanned the cluster of trees. "How much time do you think we have before the Huns get here?"

"Maybe an hour? Less?" Luther laughed wildly. "We're going to have company, Tim. What can we do to get ready for them? Too bad Maura's not here. She could make tea." His shoulders shook but not from laughter.

"Look, old man." Tim put his hand on Luther's arm. "I can't promise we'll get out of this but we've got Someone on our side. I accepted Jesus and asked God to be with me out here. God's a lot stronger than all our enemies put together." A faint stirring inside made him add, "Now that we've quit fighting each other, doesn't it make sense that we — with God's help — make a good fight of staying alive?"

"Yeah, except you and God are going to have to do most of it. I'm no use right now." Luther closed his eyes and his face twisted.

One hour later German soldiers swarmed over the little hill and swept into the area like buzzards to a battlefield. They examined the corpses and talked in their heavy language, their weapons ready against danger. Inch by inch, foot by foot they came to the quiet stand of trees and inspected the ground beneath them. Apparently satisfied, they moved on in the direction company D had fled the night before. Minutes passed; all remained still. Then a grimy, tattered figure slid down from the shelter of the tallest tree in the little grove and raced to the end of the little hill. Like a marmot digging a home, Tim threw aside dirt clods and clumps of grass once he'd dragged aside an innocent-looking log.

Would Luther be alive?

Intense blue eyes glared at Tim. Luther coughed, choked, and crawled out of his temporary grave. "Five minutes more and I'd have suffocated." He wiped dirt from his lips and spat. A reluctant grin erased his anger. "You did what you had to do. I couldn't have perched in a tree with this ankle, but I'll tell you one thing, Timothy Wainwright. The next time I'm underground, I'd better be dead!" He spat again. "When the Germans charged over the hill I knew I'd had it. Guess there was no reason for them to suspect a living soldier in his right mind would hang around here."

"Besides, your end of the hill didn't appear to have been disturbed," Tim pointed out, but a little frown crossed his face. "Luther, can you walk some? I'll carry you all I can but we may have a long march ahead of us."

Luther grimly stuck out his hand and wrung Tim's when the younger man extended his own. "I'll do it if it kills me." He reached for his homemade crutch and hobbled toward Tim, his face contorted with pain. "Like I said before, now's the time for that God of yours to come through."

14

Every bit of woods lore Tim and Luther knew from Dale days served them well in their flight. Cut off from company D, they decided to head west: West was the only direction from which they heard no sounds of fighting. Besides, the Germans would expect anyone with the Allies to try and rejoin their company. Tim felt pretty sure they'd left no sign. He'd played cowboys and Indians enough to learn ways to obliterate tracks. A branch quickly brushed over the ground would be enough unless a professional tracker came after them and he doubted that would happen.

Luther stubbornly refused to let his physical condition hold them back. He insisted on keeping up long after a lesser man would have stumbled and fallen. For the first time, Tim gave thanks for his stepbrother's tenacity. Lives were at stake. Even when Luther babbled with fever and Tim carried him until his diminished strength could take them no farther, Luther's lucid periods made it all worthwhile. So did the babbling. Time after time, Tim's heart raced when he learned Luther's story for the first time.

No wonder Luther had acted as he did! He'd been sent to Dale by relatives who had no use for him. Justin Farrell had promised the eighteen-year-old boy a bright future because long ago he and Luther's father had made a marriage pact for their children. Smarting under the knowledge his own family didn't want him, Luther determined to take control of Dale by using Justin's influence.

Hope in all her fourteen-year-old innocence proved to be everything her father promised and more. Luther's misery lifted when he first saw her — and increased when he met Timothy. Sometimes almost incoherent, Tim still caught enough to realize what a blow it was to discover the warm brother-sister relationship between Tim and Hope that left Luther an outsider *again*. His twisted thinking led him to believe that the more he discredited Tim, the better his own chances for success would be. Instead, his antics enraged Hope to the point of scorn and Luther's only reward lay in seeing Tim punished for mischief he didn't do.

If Tim needed to have his eyes opened

wider about Justin's Machiavellian hand, Luther's mental wanderings did the job. The whole plot and use of powerful connections to get Luther into command of company D came out in sordid detail. Tim helplessly fought waves of disgust and anger, praying for release from those same feelings that drained him of energy to go on. Luther's condition worsened and Tim took refuge in a deserted barn. He managed by scouring the area to find a few vegetables. When they ran out, he killed barn mice and thanked God for them. Day and night the thought drummed in his head that he must get Luther well enough to tell him about Jesus, even if neither of them ever made it home.

The period of rest helped. One late afternoon Tim roused from an uneasy sleep feeling he was being watched. Springing to attention, he slumped back when Luther quietly said, "How long have we been here?"

Tim shook his head. Time meant nothing in their situation.

"You kept your promise." Luther ran his hand over his now-bearded chin. Rays of sunlight poured in through a broken window.

Tim raised an inquiring eyebrow. "Did you ever think I wouldn't?"

"No."

A spark of feeling that had never before existed between the two smoldered. Luther's next words added fuel to the tiny flame. "Even back home, I knew you'd never lie."

With a silent cry for help, Tim looked deep into the hollow eyes across from him. "When I found you, you said you'd prayed for me to come. Did you mean it?"

Luther lay staring far beyond Tim. His eyes betrayed the turmoil within. The pungent barn odor and even the warmth of sunlight grew insignificant. "I meant it — more than anything in my life."

"But why?" Tim cried, unable to comprehend this new and strange side of Luther. "Even if you asked God for help —" He took a long, quivering breath. *Why did you ask Him to send me?*"

Bitterness settled in the freshly etched lines in Luther's face. "Think Sam or Grampaw or Kincaid would care if I lived or died?" His lips turned to a snarl. "I can't blame them. I just thought if things had been different, we could have been brothers." He turned his head but not before Tim caught the glitter in his blue eyes. "I didn't have much hope you'd come but I had to ask. . . ."

Tim sat speechless. Every poignant facet

of Luther's life that had poured out of a semiconscious, tortured mind rose and blended into realization. *We could have been brothers.* Tim leaped to his feet and bolted from the old barn. For hours he paced the area, never going far from where Luther lay. Justin Farrell had so much to answer for and the crux of all the sad past rested on Luther's belated admission.

When he rejoined Luther, Tim knelt by him and said, "It isn't too late."

Luther didn't hesitate. His face flamed with renewed courage. "Do you mean that?" His thin hand clutched Tim's arm.

"With all my heart." Freedom he had never known poured through Tim like a flooded river. He bent nearer. "Luther, there's just one thing —"

Some of the sick soldier's radiance evaporated. Apprehension shone clear in his face and the way he started. "Is it — Hope?"

Tim shook his head. "Not Hope the woman. Hope for eternity." He paused. "We're going to get out of here and go home if we possibly can. If we don't, I'd sure be proud to make my longest and last journey right alongside of you."

Luther relaxed and an unexplainable look crossed his face.

"The only thing is, if you don't admit

you're a sinner and call on God to save you, we can't do it. God loves us, and everyone, so much He let Jesus come to earth and live and die and be resurrected so we could too." Tim's voice broke. "Luther, wouldn't this be the smartest thing you could do right now?"

Luther's lips moved. Tim had to lean close to hear. "I already did. Back in the trench when I asked Him to send you."

Amazed, Tim rocked back on his heels.

"I know I acted rotten later, grabbing your weapon, trying to make you promise you wouldn't leave me." He hesitated and dark red crept into his pale face. "I'll never know if it was from fever, like you said, or because I turned yellow. I did mean it about confessing my sins, though, and asking for-giveness. I-I couldn't be sure He really heard until you came. Just now when you said we'd be brothers, I knew you'd forgiven me." His voice shook. "I knew then God had too."

Tim wordlessly gripped Luther's hand. A surge of energy he hadn't felt since high school days exploded in him. "That's just what we needed! *Thank God.* Nothing can hold us back now." He wanted to cheer and shout.

"Tim. . . ."

"Yes?"

Luther waved toward their crude surroundings then pointed to his foot. "All this, it's been worth it. But why did God have to bring us halfway around the world before we would accept Him? We can't say we didn't know about Him back home."

"Maybe because we were too busy wanting our own way to listen. The day I first left for Camp Lewis Hope pleaded with me to accept Jesus. Now she may never even know that I did." The desire to put his head in his hands and bawl like a two-year-old almost overwhelmed Tim.

"She'll know." Luther grimaced and propped his shoulders against a mound of dirty hay. "Write it in that little book you wear inside your shirt."

Tim's hand flew to his New Testament. "How did you know about this?"

Luther dropped his head and stared at the barn floor. "She talked about it in one of your letters I read." His lips tightened. "Another thing for you to forgive."

"Did you save them?" Tim managed to get out, desperately trying to overcome the remaining anger he felt.

"I didn't dare." Miserable blue eyes gazed into dark ones unflinchingly. "I'll tell you this, though. If I had the love of a woman like Hope, I'd be a different person. She's

213

like your mother." If he noticed Tim's automatic tensing he didn't mention it. "Maura used to talk about your mother and Hope's mother too. I never knew mine."

"I know," Tim blurted but wished he'd kept still.

"I figured I talked some during the fever." Luther shrugged. "It doesn't matter. It's all in the past." He shifted positions and lightened their conversation. "What's on the menu tonight? Mice or mice?"

Tim welcomed the deliberate change of subject. As Luther said, why berate the past? Their uncertain future offered enough choice of topics. "I think we'll have mice."

"How long has it been since you heard the sound of guns?" Some of Luther's officer training surfaced in the question.

"Not for a couple of days, until earlier today." Tim's eyes flashed. "I have a feeling we'd better be on the move if you're able to make it."

"We'll make it." Luther hoisted himself to his feet and looked down at his filthy clothes in protest. Even quick dips of whatever streams they'd crossed hadn't rid the travelers of their grime. "Ugh, the Germans could smell us coming a mile off." He held his nose.

"A couple of skunks in U.S. uniforms."

Tim laughed then regretted it. How often he and the others had considered Luther just that. A quick glance showed that Luther hadn't heard the sobriquet. Tim breathed a sigh of relief. When you bury the past some grim reminders of those unhappy days always stay uncovered.

"Feel like a bath?" Tim asked.

"Sure, but how?"

"There's enough water in the horse trough that hasn't leaked out after the last rain to help some." Tim helped Luther out of his ragtag officer's uniform and outside. "Try and keep your foot out. I'll help you."

"Feel like a little baby," Luther grumbled when he was half in, half out of the trough. Heavy sweat stood on his forehead by the time they finished but Luther said, "At least we can stand each other for a while," and sat in the sun to dry. "Climbing back into that uniform's about more than I can stomach."

"You don't have to." Tim soberly stepped back into the barn. "I've been saving these since we got here. Found them the first day." He held up clean uniforms.

"What are you, a magician?" Then Luther's body jerked. "Those are *German* uniforms!"

"I know. There had been a battle not far from here. I washed them as best I could."

His mouth compressed. "Their owners didn't need them." His insides twisted, remembering the early morning he found the dead soldiers. One looked like a younger edition of Luther, only with blond hair bloodied and his sightless blue eyes fixed in death.

Luther licked his lips. "You didn't find Allies?"

Tim shook his head. "If we had dead or wounded they would have been taken away. Besides, we may be glad these are German uniforms before we get out of this place. I have a feeling those guns I heard this morning aren't ours."

After a restless night Luther pronounced himself fit to travel. "Maybe we can find better accommodations," he joked. "I hate to complain but a steady diet of mice is leaving me afraid to meet up with any cats that may be left in France!"

They agreed to do as they'd done before: Travel by night, using the stars and instinct to guide them and hide out by day in whatever cover they might find. They discussed changing their direction and swinging north in a wide circle to see if they could meet up with company D and decided to make that decision later. The main thing now was to simply stay alive. The invading armies and fleeing French forces had left slim pickings behind. Starvation had to be taken into account, perhaps even more than capture, although the very word left them silent.

For every plus there was a minus. After Luther's ankle and foot had healed to the point where he could walk on it, they stumbled into a small band of soldiers. In the resulting confusion before they could silently melt back into the night a shell exploded. The world went black for Tim. "Luther, I can't see," he whispered low. He could feel blood pouring down his face. *Dear God, had he been blinded?*

Instantly Luther grabbed Tim's arm and guided him under cover, keeping low, forcing Tim on with talonlike fingers. They ran over rough terrain, taking advantage of the night, until Luther ordered a brief halt and bound Tim's head with a strip torn from his shirt. "Can't do anything else until it's light. Don't dare strike a match," he muttered. Minutes later they resumed their flight, again using time-worn ways of the woods.

By murky dawn Luther examined Tim's face. "Can you see anything?"

"No. I can't even open my eyelids." Tim kept his voice even but shock left him trembling.

"This may hurt."

Tim gritted his teeth. "Do what you have to." A quick, painful tug and Tim exclaimed, "I can see a little light with my right eye." He braced himself. "Do the left."

"How's that?" Luther asked when he'd opened Tim's left eye.

"Blurry, but I can see. What happened?"

"Looks like you may have taken shrapnel, except it must have glanced. There's a furrow across your forehead, shallow but it bled a lot. Your eyelids are so swollen and covered with dried blood it's hard to tell but I don't think your eyes themselves are affected." Luther poured a little brackish water from his canteen and washed Tim's wound and his eyes.

"Everything's still kind of fuzzy." Tim tried to open his eyes wide but they didn't want to go. "Well, looks like you're going to be the eyes of our little expedition."

"Just as you were the legs when I needed them," Luther said hoarsely. "Stay under this brush. I think I saw a peasant's hut off to the left. Let me check it out and see if anyone's there."

"Be careful," Tim whispered and strained to see Luther but his eyes hurt too much. *God, please let Luther be right. Don't let me be blinded. We've come so far. Help us home.*

What seemed an eon later, Tim awoke to

find a strong hand over his mouth. Luther loomed above him, his face like a thunder-cloud. "Don't make a sound. That hut's filled with Germans. They came just after I got outside and hidden. I've been lying under a bush for hours. They don't act sus-picious but who knows?" He shrugged de-feated shoulders. "Thought it would never get dusk so I could come back. I even won-dered if you'd think I deserted you." Pain crept into his eyes and bore mute witness to the hurtful notion.

"I know better." Tim struggled up. Be-tween the twilight and his own impaired vi-sion, Luther's face wavered. "Now what?"

"We have to get out of here as quietly and quickly as we can. On our bellies until we're into the woods. I'll go first. You hang onto my boot with one hand so you'll be right be-hind me. Once we reach the trees we have a chance but not before. Ready?"

The hollowness in Tim's stomach didn't all come from hunger. Through dry lips he mur-mured, "Ready. Don't forget, God's with us."

"Yeah, but He wants us to do what we can too." Luther bellyflopped to the ground and the most arduous journey they'd ever at-tempted began, a nightmare of stamina over incalculable fear.

An inch at a time, the brothers worked

their way across the open space, grateful for the moonless night. Hampered by Tim's firm grasp on his boot, Luther still attempted to choose the smoothest path. Tim knew how the still-tender foot must be taking the brunt of their snakelike progress where every moment brought the danger of detection.

Both men lay gasping by the time they reached the frail shelter of thicket that edged an upward sloping hillside covered with forest. Luther hesitated only for a moment. "Now we can climb until we give out. By then we should be high enough to get a view in the morning of the hut or what's happening down here. Can you go on?"

"With the help of God, yes." Timothy gulped in fresh night air and prepared to follow. "I'll hook my fingers over your belt."

All that night Luther and Tim alternated climbing with brief rest periods. Hope rose with every step. It seemed unlikely the Germans would choose to go up a mountainside without good cause and what would they gain by storming an unoccupied mountain? Still the weary soldiers kept their voices low. Just after daylight Luther grunted and said, "We should be safe here but we'd better take turns standing guard." He yawned. "Do you want first watch or second?"

Timothy never had the chance to answer.

A band of fierce-faced men in tattered clothing leaped from bushes and trees and fell on the two exhausted soldiers. Their eyes gleaming with triumph, they encouraged each other in a foreign tongue. Tim saw Luther go down from a blow. Then all was velvet blackness.

15

Hope Wainwright straightened from her cramped position above the hospital bed. Bone-tired, still she smiled at the pain-filled face looking up at her. "You're going to be all right, you know." Thank God for that. Seeing Tad Wilson shattered in body and unbeaten in spirit had been the hardest task Hope faced in her months as a volunteer nurses' aide. The reality of war lay embodied in the boyish face and knowing eyes.

"Is there any word from Tim or Sam? My outfit never got close enough to theirs so we could jaw." Regret deepened the lines in his forehead. "As soon as Doc lets me out of here I'm going back. The job isn't over."

Hope shook her head. "It's been months since I heard from Tim and the Johnsons say there's no word from Sam either." She sighed sadly. "At least, they must be all right or we would have been informed by the government." Her lips quivered and she stared with unseeing eyes at the spotless hospital walls. "I keep hoping it will end soon. It's been months since President Wilson announced his Fourteen Points for peace in early January."

"Only to have Germany launch *three* huge offensives on the western front in late March," Tad grimly reminded her and moved to a more comfortable position. "I guess their getting parts of Finland, Poland, the Baltic States, and a lot of other land from Russia in the eastern front freed more German troops to fight in the west." He looked somber. "I can't blame Russia for signing the treaty. They've taken a terrible beating. So have France and England." He restlessly turned his head on the pillow. "We've gotta stop them! Paris got bombarded so hard with Germany's 'Big Berthas' from about seventy-five miles away I thought it was a goner." A grin of pure satisfaction erased the wrinkles from his face.

"We showed them at Château-Thierry, though, and in the second Battle of the Marne. General Foch and the Allies have been steadily pushing the Germans back." He closed his eyes for a moment. "I guess maybe I won't feel good enough to go back after all. The newspaper you brought me said the Allies are gathering by the thousands near the Argonne Forest, 900,000

U.S. soldiers alone! We'll show old Kaiser Bill." The light of undimmed patriotism burned deep in his eyes and lit a candle in Hope's heart.

"Get some sleep, Tad." She smoothed his rough hair back and plumped his pillow. Heartsore and weary, Hope almost stumbled from the room. She leaned against the wall for support, chastising herself for weakness in the face of the grueling path Tad and so many others traveled back from death's door. If only word would come of Tim and the others! Perhaps she should go ahead and enroll in regular nurses' training. Fall classes would begin soon. Hope slowly walked to the window and looked out. Already leaves had begun to turn. What would September 1918 bring? To her, to Dale, to the world? More bloodshed? More heartache and uncertainty and prayers . . . or peace and the return of the boys? In the long months of waiting even Luther's heckling didn't concern her. He was simply one of Dale's own, fighting in a far country so women like her could be free.

Hope no longer worked at the library. Grace Forsythe forbade it. "You are far more needed where you are. Even when all you do is bring fresh water — and I know your duties are far more demanding than that — you can bring hope and courage to those broken young men coming home. Don't be afraid to smile. More healing comes from a cheerful countenance than we'll ever know."

Then Grace's blue eyes darkened. "When you're so tired you think you can't go on and when you face sights that make you blanch, remember that whatever you do for the least of these, you do for Jesus. I only wish I were young and strong so I could be there too!" The cry from her heart wrapped itself around Hope.

"There are many ways to fight and win a war," she reminded gently. "Just being in the library and helping people find a way to escape into a happier world through a book is important. So is my knowing when I get home, I have a hot meal waiting."

Rumors flew wildly in Dale concerning the fighting overseas. Justin Farrell, grimmer and thinner than ever, withdrew even more into himself and walked the town with his head high but a look in his eyes that betrayed his fear for Luther. Dale had long since stopped gossiping about Hope living with Grace. More important things occupied people's minds. News accounts of a great Allied victory ahead on 26 September caused hearts to swell.

"It's begun," Hope told Tad when she went on duty. She held up a local special edition with blazing headlines:

MAJOR ALLIED OFFENSIVE IN THE ARGONNE/MEUSE RIVER AREA

Tad almost snatched the paper. His eyes gleamed. "I knew it! We've got them on the run." The paper fell and he grabbed both of Hope's hands.

"If I'd known what kind of treatment you offer here, think I'd have let them keep me in the military hospital so long?" A familiar voice drawled from the doorway.

Hope whirled. Her glad cry mingled with Tad's. "*Sam Johnson!*" She ran to the haggard man on crutches and impulsively hugged him. "You're home!" She anxiously looked him over. "Are you all right?"

"Sure." His eyes glowed with pleasure and his freckles stood out. "No German machine gunner's killing me off." He swung onto the bed. "How are you doing, buddy?"

"I'll be outta here in a few days." Tad's eagerness shone in his eyes. "When did you get back?"

"Aw, a while back." Sam was evasive and glanced sideways at Hope.

Her heart shot to her throat. "Tim, is —
was he all right?"

Every trace of color fled from Sam's face.
He looked like an old man. "Last I knew he
was." He shifted on his crutches. "I hate to
tell you but maybe it's easier coming from
me. Tim's been missing ever since I got
hurt."

"*Missing?*" Tad sat up straight, then
slumped back when Hope sank into the
chair next to the bed. "Now, Miss Hope, lots
of guys get mislaid over there. I did and a
couple of days later they found me. . . ."

Hope barely heard him. So it *had* come,
the word she'd dreaded from her last parting
with Tim, her husband. Could hearts bleed
from sheer pain? "Tell me, Sam," she
pleaded.

"Like Tad says, missing may not be so
bad. We were together in a trench when we
got hit, talking about home." Sam took a
deep breath and a little color returned to his
face. "The next thing, *bang!* It sounded like
the whole world blew up. I can't remember
much more except that Tim scooped me up
like a newborn calf and got me back from
the trench and to help. I had a bumpy ambulance ride and woke up in a field hospital
with a busted head and some shrapnel in
one thigh." He paused and licked his dry

lips as if reliving the hellish night.

Hope clenched her fingers until the nails bit into the palms of her hands, willing him to go on, afraid of what he'd say.

"Some time later, I don't know when, Sergeant Kincaid and Grampaw showed up at the hospital. They said that when they were ordered to retreat, Tim stayed behind. They didn't realize it until afterward, in all that confusion. There's something else."

"What?" Had she screamed? Hope wondered.

"Tim isn't the only one missing. No one saw Luther Jones and a few days later when company D went back for the dead, they found no sign of either." He avoided Hope's gaze.

"Then Tim ain't dead!" Tad cried. His face flamed. "Betcha he and Luther are somewhere in France right now, maybe holed up an' hurt."

"But they hate each other!" Hope didn't think she could stand this final agony. "They always have." She fought hot tears.

"Think that would keep Tim from helping Luther if he found him hurt?" Tad said scornfully.

His faith brought a burst of strength to the distraught girl. Sam affirmed it. "I gave you the bad news first. The good news is that

228

weeks ago Tim found God on the battle-field. He's a Christian, Mrs. Wainwright. A real one." Sam's face changed. "I'd have given up a lot of times if it hadn't been for Tim."

Hope couldn't say one word for the joy that went through her.

"There's something else." Sam really smiled for the first time. "When the fighting started hot and heavy, guess who came down off his high horse and bellied into the trenches with the rest of us?"

"Not Luther!" Tad's eyes threatened to pop from his skull.

"The same." Hope could see how much Sam was enjoying himself. "Grampaw said he reckoned some of being around the men of Dale had rubbed off but whatever changed him, he sure fought fierce. He was at the far end from Tim and me, beneath a little hill. The way I figure is either he or Tim got hit and the other one stayed behind to help."

Sam drew himself to full height. A look of pleasure lent sparkle to his worn face. "Now Dad's gonna drop me off at Justin Farrell's bank so I can give our leading citizen an earful." He threw a meaningful glance at Tad, who grinned in return, then he limped toward the door. "Don't you worry a-tall," he ordered Hope. "One of these days the war will be over and when it is, I expect Tim and maybe even Luther to come crawling out of wherever they are and head for home. See you later."

Hope's eyes stung at the gallantry of the man on crutches, but Tad said, "Why don't you go with him?" Then he shook his head. "Naw, wait a little while and let your father chew on what Sam has to say."

Hope came out of her trance and hurried out into the hall and after Sam. She caught up with him on the hospital porch. "Do you know if Tim got my letters? Your father said those from you appeared to have been opened and I haven't heard from Tim for months."

"I'm sorry to say mine looked the same way," he told her. His eyes flashed. "He never doubted you though. He knew why he didn't hear. One other thing, in case you wonder. Tim didn't accept Christ just 'cause you wanted him to. It's real and between him and his Lord."

"Thank you, Sam," Hope whispered. "And oh, God bless you, dear friend." She watched him slowly make his way out to his father's old car. Regret that Tim had faced his trials without even the comfort of her letters surged into a tide of gladness. No matter what happened in the uncertain future, someday she would again see her beloved.

This blessed assurance carried her through the dragging weeks of September, all of October, and into gray November. Bulgaria surrendered during the Allied victory in the Argonne Forest with Germany on the edge of collapse through October. Countless riots and demands for peace forced Kaiser Bill to give up the throne on 7 November after the German Navy had mutinied. He fled to the Netherlands. General Foch and an Allied delegation met with German representatives in a railroad car in the Compiègne Forest in northern France.

Early on the morning of 11 November 1918 the Germans officially surrendered. General Foch ordered all fighting to stop at 11 A.M. The "War to end all wars" was over.

The world went mad. Every city, village, and hamlet in the United States celebrated the Armistice. Church bells pealed, whistles shrieked, small boys beat tin pans, and normally sober citizens danced in the streets. Drums and washboards and boilers and stovepipes provided a steady *thump, thump* to the screaming and tears.

"The war is over!" a stentorian voice bellowed from the middle of Main Street and

countless voices chanted the cry. Hope watched the fire wagon and Mr. Wilson's milk wagon with its empty cans clatter down the street. Unbridled tears poured from Mr. Wilson's eyes. Miss Hattie hugged Reverend Slater and Maura danced an Irish jig in front of the entire town!

Yet for Hope, Justin, Grampaw's family, and others who waited, the war was not ended and would not so long as one of their own remained overseas or not accounted for.

The one strangely missing in the jubilance stood partially hidden behind a fine lace curtain in his big home watching his town and secretly hating them all. Who cared that the fighting had ceased when the only one who really mattered to Justin had vanished in the mists of war? The banker's soul was as cold as iron. Even the faith of his fathers that he observed and upheld did little to temper the bitter moment. Why had he agreed to let Luther go? Better a live son than a dead hero, and, according to Sam Johnson, Luther had given his best.

For hours Justin stood there while night ended and a new day began. Along with the shouting, the hastily assembled town band's rousing rendition of Sousa's "The Stars and Stripes Forever" and the continual proclamation, "The war is over!" almost drove Justin mad. He longed to rush into the streets and proclaim it a lie. Not until Luther came home would the war end, and perhaps not even then.

At last Justin faced his deepest fear. Luther's safety, his very life in all probability, rested in the hands of the boy-turned-man he had wronged. Justin had listened silently to Sam's story, fixing his gaze on the other's face and drawing from him every ounce of information he carried or suspected. He even shook hands in parting and refused to resent the pity in the wounded soldier's eyes.

"Sam said Tim had become a Christian," Justin told the empty room. "God help my son if Sam is wrong." Blinding tears came in torrents, sliding over the craggy face. The man who had sacrificed the love Tim would have given and banished his daughter who would not bend to his will now suffered alone, clinging to the frail straw Sam Johnson offered for Luther's salvation.

Before the sounds of victory subsided, the world faced a more ruthless juggernaut than the war itself, one that claimed over twice as many lives worldwide as the estimated 8½ million of World War I. In the winter of

1918–1919 influenza raged throughout the world leaving devastation behind. Even the strongest had no defenses against it. Good nursing and the power of prayer offered the only hope.

Hope went about her hospital duties with a set face and a faraway look in her amber eyes. A hundred times Grace's reminder that when she served the least she served Jesus gave her the strength to go on. She no longer waited for word of Timothy and Luther. If they had been captured and remained alive, or if they had indeed hidden out as Sam and Ted stubbornly insisted, surely in the weeks since the Armistice word would have come.

Always in the back of her mind lay a longing, a wistful dream that one day her father would relent and welcome her back into his life. Sometimes she remembered the day she left. Maura's words, "It's his awful proudness," and later, in Grace Forsythe's quiet living room, "It's himself he has to be forgivin' first," came rushing back.

The Dale men who had gaily gone to war had come home: a few in caskets, to be mourned by the whole town; some untouched; others broken in health but not in spirit. One or two suffered shellshock and a few fought for daily breath into lungs scarred by mustard gas. To these and others Hope brought everything her name implied. She never failed to witness for her Lord and those with family members dying began to call on her when overworked Reverend Slater couldn't come. Her quiet touch and ready prayer brought comfort to sick and grieving alike and a strange feeling that each one she ministered to represented Timothy kept her going when other volunteers fell by the wayside, sick and discouraged.

On a gloomy late winter day Maura came to her. "Himself is took bad." A great compassion born of need and living with death showed in the steady Irish-blue eyes. "Will ye come?"

Hope paled. "I must." She quickly packed a few things, just enough to keep her going, and walked the long Main Street to her old home. "Will he know me?" she asked Maura.

Her faithful friend shook her head. "Nay." Her brogue sounded thicker than ever. "Perhaps it's just as well — for now. Hope, lamb, the doctor says —"

"There is no hope?"

Maura tossed her head with some of her usual independence. "I haven't been hearin' the Great Physician give such an opinion," she remarked and pulled her cape closer around her shivering body. "There, that's enough blathering. There's work to be done." She led the way up the front walk of the Farrell home and stopped and looked deep into Hope's eyes.

"I've no need to be for tellin' ye how it goes."

"No." Hope recited as if by rote. "Try and keep the fever down. If patient can get through the first week or ten days, there's a chance. Many die in the first few days."

She lost her control and gripped Maura's arm, her eyes wide with fear. "*He can't die, Maura!* Not until he's forgiven me — and Timothy. We can't let my father face God with hatred in his heart!" Her cry rang in the gray twilight, unheard by neighbors who cared and prayed for their own.

But Maura placed an arm around the trembling girl's shoulders and opened the front door. "Then we'd best be for gettin' started, hadn't we?" The closing of the door behind them sounded a death knell in Hope's heart.

16

Days and nights blended into weeks for Hope and Maura. When the overworked doctor made an infrequent visit, he simply shook his head and marveled that Justin clung to life. "Keep on with what you're doing," he gruffly ordered and rubbed red-rimmed eyes, wondering how long he could keep on before collapsing.

"How bad is it?" Maura inquired. "In Dale, I mean."

"Bad." The doctor picked up his bag. "We'll lose more to this devilish illness than we lost to war." He cleared his throat. "I'll try and come back when I can." A feeble smile brightened his worried face. "Do you know the most beautiful word in the world? *Over.* Someday this will be over, pray God. I just hope it comes soon." He wearily went downstairs and out the door to others who needed him.

Hope and Maura learned what the Apostle Paul meant when he admonished,

"Pray without ceasing."* Every waking moment, like a silver river running through a parched land, their petitions spoken and unspoken bore them up and helped them go on in the face of hopelessness.

At first Justin called out for Luther, again and again until Hope thought she would go mad. No matter how much she pressed his hand and tried to reassure him through stiff lips, his delirious gaze and restless hands never stilled. Yet as the same spirit that once brought him wealth and position now fought to keep life in his wasted body, now and then Justin cried in a low monotone, "Timothy." Once as Maura and Hope physically restrained him from thrashing in the sheets drenched with sweat, he whispered, "Must tell Timothy." The women could only guess at what demons haunted the sick man's mind.

A few times he called for Hope. On those occasions her firm grasp and clear voice penetrated his unconsciousness long enough for him to pause before continuing his cries.

"It's pitiful, that's what it is." Maura put her apron over her face one early evening after a particularly bad night and day. "To

* 1 Thessalonians 5:17(KJV)

see himself like this." The apron fell and Hope saw bright stains on Maura's cheeks, thin now instead of rosy and plump.

Hope stared straight ahead, too tired and dispirited to reply. *Could life hit any harder than it had already done?* First her own mother had been taken. Then Tim, whom she had adored. Then Luther, now Father. Grace and Maura remained, but who knew for how long? Would this terrible epidemic never cease?

She flung herself into Maura's arms. "Maura, don't leave me! You and Grace are all I have left."

"And where would I be for goin'?" Some of Maura's spunk returned. Her workworn hand stroked the golden head with its disheveled curls. "Besides, ye will always have your Heavenly Father, child."

Comfort stole into Hope's heart. But a wild cry from Justin's bedroom brought them both upright and back on duty. Burning hot, he sat bolt upright in bed crying for Luther.

"See if the doctor can come quick," Hope ordered, and seized a fresh towel. She dipped it in ice water and tried to place it over her father's face but he flung it aside. The next moment he fell back senseless. A shadow crept across his face. His eyes closed.

Hope frantically felt for a pulse and found it. "Thank God." Yet when the doctor arrived a few minutes later he shook his head. "It's the crisis and it doesn't look good." He pried open the set lips and poured in medicine. Most of it leaked out the corner of Justin's mouth. "If you can, try and get this in him, a little every hour or so. I have to tell you, it will take a miracle to save him." He sighed as he did so often these dark days and picked up his black bag. Streaks of white that hadn't been there a few months earlier shone in his hair. "I wish I could stay but at least three others need me more right now."

Hope faintly heard his heavy steps on the stairs and the opening and closing of the front door. Her pain subsided into numbness and she whispered to Maura above the still form, "It's too late, isn't it? For a miracle."

Wisdom filled her beautiful eyes. "Nay, child. Our Father often answers at the eleventh hour when things look most hopeless." She raised her head, swept a glance at the closed window, and ribbons of red streamed into her face. "Will ye be trusting me enough to take a chance?"

"With my life, Maura." Hope glanced down at her father. "And his."

"Then so much for doctor's orders. This

air's enough to kill anyone." Maura pushed up the window sash. "Keep him lightly covered," she warned and moved to another window. Soon cold air circulated through the room. Maura closed the windows, waited, and reopened them, again and again. Her efforts brought a sigh from Justin — was it a sigh of relief?

All night Maura continued her forbidden treatment and Justin was still alive when dawn came.

Thousands of miles away Timothy Wainwright awakened from strange, troubled dreams. He rubbed his eyes. *How long had he been asleep? Hadn't this happened before?* He closed his sleep-filled eyes and tried to orient himself. He remembered he and Luther had made it up the mountainside but had been attacked by strange men in tattered uniforms. He had seen Luther fall before his head exploded. When he regained consciousness, pressure on his eyes weighted the lids and he struggled then raised a hand. Bandaged! *Had his captors put his eyes out?* He shuddered.

"*Non.*" A firm voice spoke and a hand pulled his away from his bandaged eyes.

Tim's hand fell. Something rough covered him. He desperately gathered his senses.

"Luther?" He fought to sit up but the same hand pushed him back. The crisp voice rapidly spoke. Tim's heart raced. It didn't sound like the guttural German his keen ears had learned to distinguish so well. He repeated, "Luther?"

A door creaked open. The sound of many steps came near. "It's okay, Tim. Here, wait a minute."

Luther's voice. *Thank God!* He sounded cheerful so things must be all right. Tim felt layer after layer being unwound from across his eyes and around his head. He blinked when light seeped through, closed his eyes, then forced them wide.

"Can you see?"

Tim blinked again. Cleansing tears gushed away the fogginess. He looked straight into Luther's concerned face. "I never knew how beautiful that mug of yours could look, beard and all," he exclaimed and Luther shouted with laughter.

"Think I'm beautiful? You should see yourself. I've never observed a couple of shiners as pretty as yours."

"Where are we?" Tim tore his gaze free and checked out his surroundings. He lay on a pallet on a dirt floor. Curving stone arched above him and a crackling fire was contained in one corner. "A cave, for crying out loud?" Next he scanned the little group of gaunt-faced men. "Who are they? Not Germans, but then, why'd they jump us?"

The tallest of the men who still didn't reach ether Tim or Luther's height leaned over and smiled. He motioned to Luther and they propped him up against the wall with a folded coat behind him. "Les Français, we are," the man said. "Peasants, we fight."

Things began to fall into place. "French guerrillas?" Excitement drove the last of Tim's doubts away.

The man, evidently the leader of the band of peasants, raised his eyebrows and looked at Luther who nodded.

"Peasants who lost their land and weren't considered fit to fight by their country but who refuse to stay out of it." Luther smiled warmly at the leader. "Pierre," he indicated, then waved his hand at the others. "Claude, Jacques, Louis, Paul, Yves, Jean, and Antoine." Each man bowed and doffed a battered beret. "They understand English but Pierre speaks it best."

"Germans we think you are," Pierre explained. His dark eyes danced. "We see you come. *Voilà!* We leap from trees. We tie you up. Look for guns — this we find." He pointed to the stained and crumpled New

Testament lying on the ground next to Tim. "German? *Non.* English words, I read some." He shrugged. "A thousand pardons." He spread his hands wide then pointed to Luther. "When he wake up, he say you are Américain."

"They've taken care of us ever since," Luther added. "They don't have much food but have shared." He ruefully pointed to his foot. "They also did what they could for my ankle and I'll come out of it with no more than a limp." His hand shot out and fastened on Tim's arm. "We'd have both cashed in if they hadn't found us."

"How long have I been out?" Tim wanted to know.

"Long enough to scare me half to death," Luther admitted. "When they attacked you, you fell hard and banged your head pretty badly. I started to wonder if even when you woke up you'd remember anything." His laugh sounded strained. "I'm not sure how we'd have handled an amnesia victim!"

"When can we travel?" Tim snapped his head back and regretted it. The great-grandfather of all headaches pounded in his brain.

"We can't. At least, not for a long time," Luther amended. His hair shone bright gold in the firelight and he hunkered down next to Tim. "We're pretty well pinned down. Pierre and the others aren't sure that the enemy knows they're here but they scout every day and the place is surrounded. As long as we stay in the cave we're safe. Once we leave —" His expressive shrug told the rest of the story.

"They probably think we're dead. Company D and the people back home." The thought chilled Tim and he remembered Luther's comment when he scrambled out of the hillside cover about being buried alive.

"You stay with us," Pierre interrupted. "When the Germans go, we go. Too many to fight now." Hatred dulled his eyes and a general mumble of assent rippled through his men.

Later Luther whispered, "We thought we had it rough. These fellows can tell things so incredible they're almost impossible to accept. They've seen homes and families destroyed. I honestly think the only thing keeping them alive is the desire for revenge. I-I tried to tell them about God but they think He's forgotten them or He would have stopped the Germans."

Luther fell silent and Tim considered the things he'd said. *Would the day ever come when men lived as brothers instead of as adver-*

saries intent on wiping each other out forever?
His lips twisted. How could he condemn
these homeless men? Hadn't it taken a war
to bring him to his knees and heal forever
the battle with Luther?

When Tim got over his dizzy spells and
felt able to do more than lie prone, he and
Luther helped provide food for the little
band of comrades. They formed snares and
successfully trapped small animals now and
then. They lay beside a sluggish stream and
captured frogs and sometimes fish. Although they never felt full, enough strength
to keep hunting lightened their spirits. The
Frenchmen never tired of hearing about
America. Luther and Tim learned more
about France than any geography or history
course ever taught. A brotherhood grew,
strong enough to bridge the gaps left by different languages and different ways.

One afternoon Tim realized he hadn't
heard the sound of guns for days. The
others agreed and that evening two of the
men slipped away to scout the area. They
came back the next morning dirty faced but
eyes shining. "The Germans, they are gone.
The Americans, gone." They waved their
hands wildly. "Tanks broken. Guns still."

"A little longer we wait," Pierre decided.
Eternal sadness showed in his face.

Tim looked at his own clothing and felt ashamed. Once Pierre and his men discovered they had captured Americans, they burned the German uniforms and pooled the best of their own clothes for their "guests," over Tim and Luther's protests. Still, all ten men looked like scarecrows on a poor man's farm.

A few days later Pierre announced, "Tomorrow we go."

A shout went up and resounded from the cave walls. Tim caught a look in Luther's eyes that reflected his own feelings. Once away from the sheltering cave, the French peasants must go one way, the two Americans another. Would they ever meet again? Could anything the two Christians said spark interest or someday bear fruit? Tim prayed it would and found solace in Paul's letter to the Corinthians: *I have planted, Apollos watered; but God gave the increase.** During their enforced stay in the cave, Tim and Luther began to study the Scriptures and often marveled at how applicable they were even to this unnatural situation.

They did not leave the next morning as planned. The two men who had so happily returned with good news lay deathly ill. The

*1 Corinthians 3:6(KJV)

stench of vomit and the heat of fever filled the little cave.

Pierre beckoned Luther and Tim to follow him. Once outside the cave, he said quietly, "You must go. When this sickness comes, it takes many. All, maybe. Today, Claude and Antoine. Tomorrow, Pierre, Luther, Tim, n'est-ce pas?" He shrugged. "We have nothing. You have America, family. *Allez*, go." He dramatically pointed down the mountainside.

Tim whirled toward Luther for confirmation of his own heart. The look on his stepbrother's face of longing for home slowly gave way to growing determination. Tim's own heart faltered. *Could he throw away the life God had spared so many times? Did he dare risk Luther's life?* God, how could a man be asked to weigh the value of one life against the lives of others? Shame scorched him and left his face hotter than Claude and Antoine's. In God's eyes Pierre and the others were as precious as Tim and Luther. Had God allowed all that came before in order to bring His word to dying men?

"We will stay." Two voices speaking as one, choosing life eternal through the Master's service rather than life itself.

Pierre put the same proposition to Jacques, Louis, Paul, Yves, and Jean. Dark eyes flashed like sabers. Five heads shook in unison.

Pierre threw up his hands in despair. "We stay — to the death."

"To the death," the others chorused and Tim saw victory in the gallant leader's defeat.

They buried Claude and Antoine two days later, Jacques and Paul the following day, and Louis a week later. Haggard and worn, Pierre ordered the others to go.

They refused again.

Yves and Jean fell sick a few days later, then Luther. All three begged Pierre and Tim to leave. "I know you promised but someone has to go back and tell what really happened," Luther cried through his weakness. He retched again. "Tim, for my sake, for Hope's sake, for the love of God — go!"

"I cannot." He gently held Luther's shaggy head in his arms, praying that God would spare them further suffering.

Pierre and Tim remained to care for the others. Often they talked when their almost endless duties permitted and most often the talk turned to Tim's faith. Pierre had long since learned of the boyhood feud that separated the step-brothers into enemy camps as bitter as the French and Germans. Tim felt his friend's measuring look when he told how he met God on the battlefield. He didn't gloss over that moment of fierce exaltation when he knew the final confrontation with Luther had arrived, the moment of revenge.

Pierre's eyes gleamed with sympathy and moistened when Tim doggedly confessed how unworthy he felt. "Your God, His Son, died for Pierre? For Jean and Claude and the others?"

"Yes." Tim held back a rush of words that trembled on his tongue.

"*Moi,* I think about it." The first grin in days lit Pierre's thin face. "*Maintenant,* I see if the little bird or animal gets in the trap." He slipped from the cave, leaving Tim to pray with all his heart.

Just when Yves and Jean seemed better and Luther continued to hold his own, Pierre succumbed, leaving Tim to care for and feed the four men. He pushed his body beyond belief, trying to keep at least a semblance of cleanliness in the cave, attend to the men, and still find time to scavenge for food from an ever-diminishing supply. At times the only thing that kept him going was that, of the four, Luther needed him most. But the day came when he knew that unless God intervened, they'd all die — if not of influenza, from starvation.

Tim bowed and cried to his God, not on his own behalf but for the sake of his friends and brother. "They're starting to listen," he told God. "Pierre, Yves, Jean. Luther needs you, too, and so do I. Help us God. . . ." He fell into a deep sleep before he could finish.

The fire in the cave had died to a few winking embers. Yves and Jean lay in huddled positions; Luther and Pierre breathed heavily. Tim awoke feeling as refreshed as he had at Camp Lewis. How many hours or days had he slept? He stood and crossed to the others, sighed, and pulled Jean's blanket over his face. Another grave to be dug. Yves moaned and lay still but he looked cooler.

Tim passed his hand over Yves's face. *Sweat!* His fever had broken. He managed to dig a shallow grave and lay Jean's body in it and then covered it with stones. Perhaps someday if any of them lived to show the way, someone might want to reclaim the bodies.

A week later Yves could manage simple tasks so long as they didn't take much strength. Pierre and Luther both fought with all their might and inch by inch came back to life, weaker than newborn kittens but alive.

On a cold morning Tim took Yves outdoors. "We must have food. Can you go?"

"Me, I not desert," Yves said proudly and drew his thin body to the utmost of his short stature.

"It isn't deserting, Yves," Tim said simply. "There isn't any use pretending. I haven't been able to find food for three days. I've been making a broth out of leaves. We can't go on like this. It made sense to stick together before but now they're going to die if we don't get food. Please, Yves, go!" His voice cracked and broke.

Yves didn't say one more word. He merely inclined his head, slipped back into the cave for his weapon, and marched past Tim.

The day died at noon. Tim shivered in the thinnest of the blankets and fed the fire one stick at a time. Why hadn't he brought in more fuel before the fog came? Too late now, even if he had the strength. Lassitude crawled over him and the feeling that he had lost. If Yves didn't come back . . . well, what if he did? How much chance had the still-weak man of finding anything to eat in this Godforsaken land?

At the moment when Tim faced his last trial, Hope's sweet face and his voice promising her he'd come back roused him. Or had someone thrown a huge log on the fire? He was hot, hotter than he'd ever been before. Hadn't he once said he never wanted to be cold again? He laughed wildly. He had his wish. If he could just get to the mountains, just lie in the snow. But he was on a mountain, wasn't he? Could he crawl outside the cave and see if he could find snow?

With a gigantic lunge, Tim forced his body to perform a final act. "God, I did my best. I can't get Luther home, but You can — and I'll see him again someday, with You and Hope. Maybe even Pierre." He reached the edge of the cave, fell, and lay still.

"Hope?"

A voice pierced her consciousness. She looked up from where she'd fallen asleep next to her father's bedside. "Is he gone?"

"No, he's cooler," Maura told her. She pulled her robe closer. "It's morning and ye must rest."

"I can't leave him." Hope glanced at the quiet figure who scarcely breathed.

"Ye must. What good will ye be to him if ye give out or get sick, I'll be askin'?" She determinedly helped Hope up from her cramped position.

Hope found it easier to submit than protest. She meekly allowed Maura to help her undress and tuck her in and she even ate a few bites of the delicious breakfast Maura

253

quickly prepared. "I won't sleep," she predicted.

"We'll see." Maura smiled and Hope closed her eyes. For the second time that day Maura's voice shook off slumber. "Father?" she mumbled.

"Nay, it's this." Maura reluctantly extricated a telegram from her apron pocket. Eyes filled with fear, she mumbled, "I took the liberty of openin' it."

"Tell me, Maura." Hope wanted to scream. All the months of waiting and now this.

Maura raised anguished eyes toward her mistress. "It says, BRINGING TIMOTHY HOME. LUTHER."

Hope slid from her bed. "I must tell Father. At least Tim can be buried here, close to the hills he loved."

Maura looked at her strangely and Hope put both arms around the motherly woman. "It's all right. I think I knew it would be this way. It's not as if I won't see him again. We both know that." A glorified look swept over her pale face. "Perhaps this message will rouse Father. I've prayed so much for him."

All that day Hope sat by her father's bed and whenever he moved she said clearly, "Luther's coming, Father." The first few times he gave no sign he had heard but at dusk he opened his eyes.

"Luther's coming, Father," Hope repeated. A great rush of joy filled her when he feebly smiled.

He whispered just loud enough to be heard, "Timothy?"

"Luther is bringing him." Hope forced herself to smile.

Justin heaved a great sigh. "Now — I — can — sleep." Thirty seconds later he fell into his first natural sleep since he became sick.

"How can I tell him Timothy's dead?" Hope asked Maura later.

"We're not knowin' for sure he is," she reminded but her red eyes showed that to be false hope.

"If it isn't true, wouldn't Luther have worded the telegram differently?" Hope firmly pushed down the unconquerable longing that had sprung to life at Maura's statement. Better to accept things as they were and be prepared to help Father through what lay ahead.

Between Maura's secret fresh-air treatment and Luther's telegram, Justin made great strides in recovery. Long before enough time had passed for the boys' arrival, he deserted his bed and roamed downstairs freely, only stopping to rest when fatigue overcame him and the doctor called him mad to tempt a relapse. Hope tried to keep a bright face in spite of feeling the best thing life could offer just now was the chance to rest. With the epidemic subsiding, she welcomed respite from hospital duties and spent as much time with Justin as possible.

"I wronged Timothy," he told her more than once. "I let my love for one boy overrule my feelings for the other. No, I can't excuse myself on those grounds. Even before Luther came I couldn't stand not having Timothy bow to my will." His thin face flushed. "Well, things are going to be different now."

Hope longed to cry out it was too late but she couldn't.

The next evening just before dark an ambulance halted at the Farrells' front gate. Sam Johnson and his father sprang out, then Tad Wilson and . . .

"*Luther?*" Justin and Hope had gone to the window. No one came calling in Dale at suppertime unless they'd been invited. Justin brushed aside Maura who had run from the kitchen at his cry. "*Luther, my son!*" He burst out the door, off the porch, and down the path.

Hope huddled in the great hall, shivering in the cold night air that streamed through the front door. In the light of the street lamp and the shining of tears she saw her father embrace the limping man whose face shone clearly all he had endured.

"But —" Justin held his son at arm's length. "Where is your brother?" His anxious voice rang in the night.

"Oh, God," Hope prayed. "Why didn't I tell him?" Remorse filled her. How could she have been so cruel when Justin had repented and eagerly waited to welcome home his second son?

Maura gasped and turned white.

Hope turned to her for comfort but with arms of steel Maura whirled her back so she faced the open door and gate.

"He's right here." Luther's homecoming joy vanished. "And in a bad way." He turned to the ambulance and helped the Johnsons and Tad lift out a stretcher with a figure under a dark blanket.

A stretcher. Not a coffin.

Straighter than an enemy bullet Hope sped down the walk past her father. Facing Hope, Luther said, "I brought him home to you, Hope. To you and the hills and God." He reverently lowered his voice. "Once you and Maura get him back on his feet we have a long and sometimes sad story, but it has a happy ending."

A sense of wonder filled Hope at his changed tone but was lost when she bent to kiss Timothy's cold lips. He reached up and encircled her until her gold curls brushed his face. "I kept my promise, dearest." Tim jealously tore his gaze from her face long enough to make sure the eternal hills stood unchanged. "Can we go inside where there's more light? I want to see you clearly."

The stretcher bearers moved up the path, hampered by Hope, Justin, and Maura who couldn't bear to step aside. Out of the darkness into the light, they marched with Luther limping but determined to do his part.

The long war had ended. Justin Farrell's two sons had gone to war severed by hate but had come home bonded forever by God's love.

The snow-capped hills of home — and Hope — smiled down on them in benediction.

The employees of Thorndike Press hope you have enjoyed this Large Print book. All our Large Print titles are designed for easy reading, and all our books are made to last. Other Thorndike Press Large Print books are available at your library, through selected bookstores, or directly from us.

For information about titles, please call:

(800) 223-1244
(800) 223-6121

To share your comments, please write:

Publisher
Thorndike Press
P.O. Box 159
Thorndike, Maine 04986